Lt-No

LEE COUNTY LIBRARY
SANFORD, N. C.

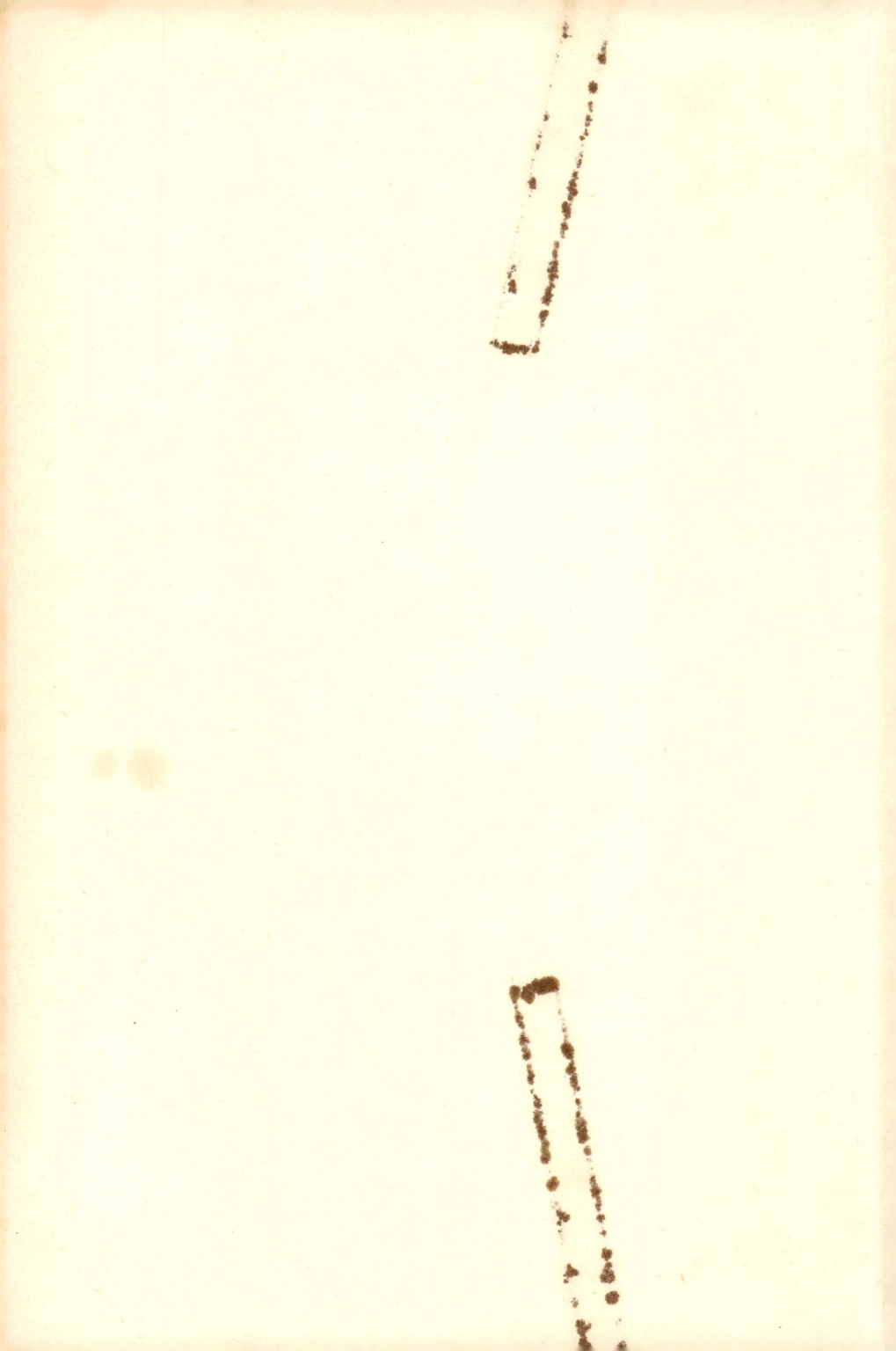

THE CHINA EXPERT

Also by Michael Delving

A SHADOW OF HIMSELF
DIE LIKE A MAN
THE DEVIL FINDS WORK
SMILING THE BOY FELL DEAD
BORED TO DEATH

THE CHINA EXPERT

Michael Delving

Charles Scribner's Sons · New York

Copyright © 1976 Michael Delving

Library of Congress Cataloging in Publication Data
Williams, Jay, 1914–
The China expert.
I. Title.
PZ3.W6739Ch [PS3545.I528455] 813'.5'2 76-23316
ISBN 0-684-14737-8
This book published simultaneously in the
United States of America and in Canada
Copyright under the Berne Convention

All rights reserved. No part of this book
may be reproduced in any form without the
permission of Charles Scribner's Sons.

1 3 5 7 9 11 13 15 17 19 H/C 20 18 16 14 12 10 8 6 4 2

Printed in the United States of America

All characters and incidents in this book are fictitious, as is the organization called *Shih P'ang,* and any resemblance to real persons, living or dead, is coincidental.

THE CHINA EXPERT

Chapter 1

End of June, a bright, clear, cloudless day of the sort which in New York would be thought of as mildly cool, but which was received by Londoners with gratitude as a heat wave. Marius, walking across Berkeley Square, looked with amusement at the youths stripped to the waist who sunned themselves on the grass, the girls in summery dresses seated demurely beside them with their faces turned skyward. There are few things more provocative, thought Marius, approvingly, than a woman's leg bent to make the thigh plumper, the knee more rounded, the curve of the calf more pronounced, particularly with the folds of a light skirt gathered chastely about the hips. I might be tempted to sit down and start a conversation, relying on my attractive American accent, if it weren't for lots 196 and 220.

He stepped off the curb, glaring belligerently at an approaching taxi so that it slowed and let him get across to Bruton Street. His thought had wandered naturally to the memory of Mei. She had delicious legs, and the slit skirt of the *ch'i pao* she always wore showed them tantalizingly. It had been four months since last he had seen her, dining in the Mustard Seed Garden. She had been with a round-faced, spectacled man who, seeing them exchange looks, had said something to her and then bowed politely to Marius. The sight of her with someone else had given Marius such a pang of unexpected jealousy that he had lost his appetite. He had thought that was all over and done with. It *was* over, and yet, a warm day, the scent of green in a London square, the glimpse of girls' legs, had filled him with wistfulness and made him feel the cold touch of loneliness once more. He shook his head. Busy as he was, well-known, well-liked, one of the top dealers in Chinese works of art, it was sheer nonsense; loneliness was for adolescents. From the corner of Bond Street he could see the familiar arched entrance of Sotheby's, and in a moment he would be among friends and rivals.

The small basement sale room on the St. George's Street side was crowded, and Marius, passing behind the chairs to get to the front row seat which had been reserved for him, had to stop at every other step to answer greetings. He shook hands with Charles Redcliffe, the museum's curator of Japanese art, with the dealer Sun Chih-mo, with Tony Hardinge, the collector. A man he did not know, a tall, middle-aged fellow with a toothbrush moustache, came up to him and said, "Mr. Kagan? I wonder if I might have a word with you." "Not now," Marius said in annoyance. "See me later." The Parisian dealer Claudel nodded coldly to him. They had clashed in this very room, in January, when in the mêlée after a sale the best of a lot of album paintings Marius had bought had mysteriously vanished; he had known perfectly well that Claudel had taken it. He smiled at the Parisian now, nothing but affability, the word "prick" forming in his mind.

Tom Bridger had his briefcase on Marius's chair and stood up to wave. He was a square, stocky man, all chest and shoulders, his graying hair curling behind his ears, his smile full of teeth.

"Sorry I missed you yesterday," he said. "Mark told me you were in London. When did you get in?"

"Just yesterday morning. I came here first to take a look at the stuff and then went to the Comus and slept for nine hours. I've had a hard week."

He moved Bridger's briefcase and sat down, tucking his own case under the chair.

"Don't tell me you came just for this sale? It's mostly rubbish," said Bridger.

"No, I've got a few people to see, and a collection of bronzes to appraise, and then I'm going to Paris. My God, it's hot in here. You'd think they'd put up a fan, at least."

"They like to keep it snug." Bridger grinned, dropping into his own chair which crackled horribly. "You heard what happened to me in New York?"

"I heard you had some money stolen."

"No, no, nothing like that. Right after the sale that morning, I sold a few things—you remember that Hokusai painting I showed you?"

"The *Hotei?*"

"That's it. And some other things. I had forty thousand dollars in my case. I took a taxi to the *Soupière* to have dinner, went into the restaurant, and then suddenly realized I'd left my case in the cab."

"My God! What'd you do?"

"We had the police in—they're marvelously efficient, your New York cops—they checked the hack stands and worked all night, but they never found a thing. It was a blow."

Marius shook his head. "What a damn shame. Of course, I love your saying how efficient the cops are when they don't find anything. Isn't that the way things are, these days? It seems to me the whole world is full of efficiency which leads nowhere except to the scrap heap."

"You Americans always exaggerate," said Bridger. "It's one of your charms. It was my own fault for being such a bloody idiot. But then, I was tired. I'd been in Honolulu two days before, and when I got back to New York I'd forgotten about the time change. I lost eight hours and messed up all my appointments."

He laughed; he had an infectious laugh, which had more than once clinched a sale. "By the way," he went on, glancing sidelong at Marius, "I saw an old friend of yours a few days ago. Mei Yuan."

"Is that so?" Marius said, trying not to sound interested. "Where was this?"

"At a party Tony gave. I was there with an absolutely smashing bird, a model—"

"You're becoming the world's champion bird-watcher, aren't you?"

"I don't waste time watching, Marius. Anyway, she came up to me and said, 'I'm Yuan Mei, I don't know whether you remember me, I used to be a friend of Marius Kagan's.' I said I did, and how could anyone forget her? She has one of those pure jade Chinese faces, hasn't she?"

"What was she doing at Tony's?" Marius said, slumping down in his seat as if bored.

"She was there with some bloke, a Taiwan businessman, a friend of Sun Chih-mo's, I gathered. She said he wanted to meet me, was interested in Japanese prints. Then she asked me if I'd seen you recently. I got the idea she'd started the whole conversation just to lead up to that. You know how devious these Orientals are."

"Inscrutable is the word you're looking for."

"That's right. I said I'd seen you in New York in April, and she wanted to know how you looked and what you were up to. I'm not boring you, am I?"

Marius grunted.

"That's all over, is it?" Bridger asked, his tone suddenly sympathetic.

Marius sat up straight. "Long ago," he replied. "Look, Mark's here." The auctioneer had come up to the podium and was shuffling papers; he smiled and nodded at Marius. "Let's meet later," Marius said to Bridger. "What about dinner?"

"Fine. It's my turn, though, I think."

"No, you took me to the *Soupière*. What about coming over to the Comus at seven-thirty?"

Mr. Nakamura, a dealer from Kyoto, was leaning forward on Bridger's other side, smiling and bowing, and Marius bowed back.

"Oh, nice to see you, Mr. Kagan. You are here for a few days?"

"Good to see you, too. Yes, I'll be here until the end of the week."

The auctioneer, looking about him like a schoolteacher waiting for the class to come to order, said, "Very well, ladies and gentlemen, if you please. Lot number one—"

Marius hardly listened. The first hundred lots or so were Japanese prints, not for him, they were Bridger's meat. Lot 220 was primarily what he had come for. It was a small, free landscape, an album leaf mounted as a *kua chou,* or hanging painting, by the seventeenth-century master Chu Ta (although with Chinese paintings there remained always the faint shadow of doubt). And lot 196 was interesting, a two-fold Momoyama screen for which he had a customer, although it was Japanese work, if he could get it cheaply enough. There were several other lots as well, but he had plenty of time.

So she had been asking about him, had she? She hadn't forgotten, any more than he had. But it was over, it had to be, they would have ended by tearing each other to pieces.

He had first met Mei at a New Year's banquet given by Paul Li at his restaurant, the Mustard Seed Garden. Li, an avid collector of porcelain, invited his friends every year and that year it happened that Marius was in London. The guest list included scholars, connoisseurs, dealers, about equal numbers of Chinese and Westerners, all as eager to sample the stuffed, glazed chicken and fish in plum wine sauce as to look at Li's latest acquisitions. Dr. Yang had introduced Marius to a very attractive woman with a round, merry face. She had black hair cut short, very white teeth, smooth thick skin with a golden tone like—as Bridger had said—jade, and a handsome figure which the green silk of her dress showed to advantage. She was interested in painting, a collector on a small scale, and they had spent some time talking. Her comments were more than simply intelligent and revealed wide reading and an impressive background; her father had been a noted collector. After dinner, they had settled into a corner to talk and before they parted she had invited him to her flat to see her collection.

She was, he learned, the widow of a well-to-do Hong Kong importer. After her husband's death she had kept up the business from the London office. Like many Oriental women, she was older than she looked, forty-two, eight years younger than Marius; she had a son in Sussex University. Marius found her enchanting, but he kept himself very cool and polite, knowing how proud and easily offended such women could be. She seemed to like him, they met again, several times, and then, shortly before he had to leave London, they had suddenly, fiercely, unexpectedly fallen into bed together.

They had seen each other every day, Marius letting business slide until he could no longer put off leaving. They had met each time he returned to London during the next year. Once or twice, he had gone across on the slightest of pretexts, just to be with her. They had grown more and more fond of each other, and then inevitably, the question of marriage had come up.

Mei was not at all willing to leave England. Her business was there, her son, ties with her own and her husband's family, a wide circle of friends. She liked England in spite of its shortcomings which she was frank to admit, and she was by no means sure she would like America. As for Marius, although he thought of himself as deeply rooted nowhere, he could not simply transport his center of operations out of New York, where most of his best customers were. He had no shop but worked out of the small, comfortable house he had bought on East 68th Street before prices became astronomical, and he felt himself at the center of things, able to get to Asia or Europe with equal facility. Furthermore, although he enjoyed being in London, he did not really like England. He felt its economy was collapsing and that it was only a matter of time before it fell into the hands of extremists on the Right or the Left. Even more to the point, English taxes were too high, and "I don't intend to go chasing around the way I do just to fill the pockets of the tax collector," he said.

Mei would not be moved. "I don't want be your London girl friend," she said, firmly, and added, in Chinese, "The time for playing with sex is over. I am an old-fashioned person, and if I can't live a serious life with you, I'd rather have nothing." She had her business face on, cool and impassive. "You understand?" she said, in English.

"I understand," said Marius, equally coldly. "Goodbye."

It hadn't ended there, however, but later, after many reconciliations, after much discussion, after many tears, nearly six months later. But Marius could not come to London without having to fight against phoning her again, and it seemed she had not forgotten him, either.

Like a true professional, his internal alarm clock jolted him out of his reverie at the auctioneer's calling lot 184. His eyes went to the catalogue on his lap. He had been turning the pages mechanically, without seeing them, and lot 184 was circled, one of the minor things he was interested in. "Various Chinese Artists: *Meijin Ranchiku Gafu:* 'Book of Orchid and Bamboo paintings . . .' " He looked up at Mark, who had just said, "Ten pounds," caught his attention, and lifted his catalogue a few inches upright. As long as he held it in that position, he was bidding. A few minutes later, the lot was knocked down to him for £30, or (he had no need to calculate for his mind automatically computed the exchange in half a dozen currencies) $64. He was back in the real world.

"I was hoping you were asleep," Bridger said.

"Americans never sleep," said Marius. "That's why we're a great nation."

The auctioneer frowned at them, for he was trying his best to flog a not very desirable item which had stopped at £8.

Marius bought two or three other things, and eventually they arrived at lot 196. Although Marius specialized in Chinese objects, particularly porcelain, he was not above buying Japanese works if they had some connection with China, or if he had a ready buyer for them. The screen now coming up was a handsome two-fold Kano school piece, a weeping cherry tree in snow on a gold background, sixteenth century, but in poor condition. If he could get it for less than $1,000, he could sell it in Paris at a reasonable profit. He waited for the first bids before entering.

It was not done among dealers to look around and see who was bidding. Nevertheless, all the professionals seemed to have antennae which told them who the opposition was, partly based on where the auctioneer was looking, or on the subtlest kind of movement nearby, since the biggest dealers often sat in the same general area. In consequence, Marius knew almost at once that Mr. Nakamura was bidding for the screen, and so was old Mr. Plaister farther along to the left.

Plaister was not serious. He collected by whim, too many different things, and he dropped out at £100 when Marius came in. Nakamura had always had a curious hysterical quality which sometimes led him to behave rashly, sometimes with excessive timidity. Today, it seemed to be the latter. He hesitated at £350 for a long time while the auctioneer coaxed him, and before he could make up his mind another bid came. It was from Claudel, who was sitting on Marius's right.

Marius bristled. It might be that Claudel really wanted the screen, but what seemed more likely was that he had come in just to annoy Marius and run him up. But perhaps, Marius thought, he really had a customer, maybe the same one Marius himself had in mind. For a moment Marius thought, Let him take it and see how he likes getting stuck with it, but then he determined to turn the tables. He kept his catalogue up. The price rose to £425.

Claudel was excitable and given to fits of temper.

When he was involved in a duel, his face grew pale and he began to sweat; he was sweating now, Marius knew. Marius had decided on £400 as his top figure, but he forgot it in the satisfaction of thinking of those drops of sweat. At 500, Claudel paused, then nodded, but at 525 he was finished. The auctioneer gave a brisk rap and said, "Kagan."

Marius sighed. He had given himself a certain pleasure, but it had been expensive. He jotted down the figure £525 and drew a thoughtful circle around it, writing *Nak* in the margin, and several question marks. Then he returned his attention to business; twenty minutes later he had lot 220, the Chu Ta painting, safely in his pocket, having driven out both his good friends, Paul Li and Sun Chih-mo, at £1,200.

When the sale ended, as Marius stood chatting amid the turmoil with Bridger who had taken the cream of the prints, someone tapped him on the shoulder. Marius turned to face the thin man with the small moustache who had accosted him earlier.

"Mr. Kagan, I'm sorry to trouble you but I'd very much like to talk to you."

He was tall, and Marius, who stood only five eight, had to look up at him. There was something faintly military about the moustache. Also, the tweed jacket he wore in defiance of the heat looked cheap. His accent was good. He might be a retired army man, maybe a county type, but if he was a collector it must be on a small scale for wealth often went with shabbiness in England, but never shoddy materials.

At the same time, looking past him, Marius saw Nakamura gathering up his briefcase. "Excuse me," he said, to the moustache. "I'll be with you in a moment."

He went over to Nakamura and gave him a small bow.

It was almost laughable how much they resembled each other. They were both short men, tan-skinned, with stiff dark hair cut short, both with a certain neatness and grace of movement. Marius's eyes, so dark brown as to be almost black, had an Oriental cast, and he had several times been mistaken for a Japanese or a Polynesian, which tickled him so much that customers who commented on it were sure of favorable treatment. He was, in fact, of Russian-Jewish descent, a third-generation American, born in upstate New York.

He said, "Mr. Nakamura, it's always a pleasure to see you. How is business?"

"Oh, things are very bad in Japan. There is not much money around any more. Still, I can't complain. And you?"

"The best things are fetching even higher prices in America. There is a great demand, especially, for good Japanese stuff, early stuff."

"Ah," said Nakamura. He sucked in a breath, showing himself about to say something delicate. *"Hai.* That was a very fine screen in spite of its condition. I thought the treatment very good, reminiscent of Munenobu. Don't you agree?"

"Well, really," Marius said, with a smile, "I am so ignorant of Japanese art, I can hardly say." The fact that Nakamura had responded to his opening told him that the other was regretting that he had dropped out of the bidding.

"I owe you a favor, you know," Marius went on. "I don't know whether you remember." He knew, of course, that Nakamura remembered everything of that sort, both favors owing and favors paid. "You were good enough to mention to Mr. Aoki that I had a certain ewer. If you are interested in the screen—"

Nakamura said, sadly, "But the price was very high."

Marius knew that Nakamura detested Claudel, who had once referred to him as *une espèce de singe*. He said, "That's true, but I was glad to take it away from *him*. I'm sure he had a customer lined up for it in Paris, and I also have a customer for it."

He could see by the faint flicker in Nakamura's face that he had a customer for it as well.

"I'll pass up my profit, however," Marius went on. "One must do things for one's friends. I can let you have it for five fifty."

"That is very generous of you."

"Not at all. A great pleasure."

They bowed and exchanged mutual compliments, and Marius turned away. He almost bumped into the moustached man who had been standing behind him.

"Sorry," Marius said. "Oh, yes, you wanted to see me, didn't you? What about?"

The other glanced cautiously around the room, although nobody was paying any attention to them. Marius grinned wryly to himself.

"I wondered if you would care to look at something," the moustached man said. "Something rather good, I think."

"Look, Mr.—um—"

"Fitzhugh."

"Yes, well, if it's an appraisal you want, they have excellent people upstairs and they'll tell you for free what you've got and about how much it's worth. I'm expensive."

"I'd rather not do that," Mr. Fitzhugh said, looking harassed. "I'd prefer to sell it privately. Your name was given to me as someone with a reputation for discretion and honesty who is also an authority on Chinese porcelain."

The words were irresistible. Even though he knew the odds were overwhelmingly in favor of the piece being Japanese export junk, Marius said, "I didn't know there was anyone who still thought of a dealer as honest. All right, let's see this porcelain. Where is it?"

"Not very far."

"What do you mean by not very far? I've got an appointment this afternoon."

"No, no, really not far, just round the corner in Maddox Street."

"Okay. I'll be with you in a minute or two."

Marius went off to the desk to arrange about picking up his purchases and having the screen delivered to Nakamura. He waved to Bridger, saying, "See you at seven-thirty," and shook hands hastily with one or two other people.

Paul Li, smiling behind scholarly glasses, said, "Now I'll have to steal the Chu Ta from you, eh?"

"Be patient, Paul. I want to enjoy it for a while myself."

"Very wise. But come and see me at the restaurant tonight."

"Not tonight, I've got a date with Tom. How about tomorrow?"

Mr. Fitzhugh's thin, drawn face could be seen over the heads across the room.

"Okay," Marius said, going to him. "Let's be off."

After the stuffiness of the sale room, the air in St. George's Street seemed beautifully fresh, the sun painfully bright. Marius, conscious of the height of the other man, deliberately held his pace down, forcing Fitzhugh to adapt to his speed.

"Are you a collector?" he asked.

"Oh, no," Fitzhugh replied, rather distantly.

"How do you come to have a good piece of Chinese porcelain, then?"

"Ah, well, I inherited it, you see. An uncle of mine died and left all sorts of odds and ends. He had been in the East, Foreign Service, you know, and picked up a lot of things. I've sold some of them, got rather badly burned over one or two bits, and a chap I showed this teapot to said he thought it was very good and I ought to see you."

"Who was this chap?" Marius asked, keeping his voice neutral.

"A man at the British Museum."

"Dr. Bright in the ceramics department?"

"Yes, that's right."

Marius puzzled over that. If Bright had actually vetted the piece it must be good. And yet, it was distinctly unusual for a curator to suggest the name of a dealer, even when, as in this case, they were friends. English museum people were very strict about avoiding any mention of prices or dealers when they examined articles for the public.

He went on, "You say it's a teapot. Is that what Dr. Bright called it?"

"Ah—actually no, I can't remember. I call it that. A sort of spout, you know," Fitzhugh said, with a vague gesture.

More and more peculiar. However, they were in Maddox Street by now, and Fitzhugh stopped before the door of one of the narrow, older buildings, once respectable flats on the fringe of Mayfair, now offices, shoestring business establishments, and cheap restaurants. He led Marius up a steep stairway to the first floor where two doors opened off the landing. One had "EDIBLE GOLD CROSSES, LTD., *D. R. Vindaloo*" lettered on it, the other "ELECTRODYNE RESEARCH CO." Fitzhugh unlocked the latter, somewhat to Marius's disappointment, and pushed it open.

There was a small outer office with a couple of chairs upholstered in sticky plastic, a desk and typewriter, but no typist, and a pair of big filing cabinets. Fitzhugh led the way through into a second, larger room furnished like a bed-sitter in a seedy lodging house. There was a cot and a washbasin, a square table with a teapot and an unwashed cup on it, a sagging armchair, a small bookcase full of paperbacks, and a mammoth old-fashioned chest of drawers much scratched. Two grimy windows looked out into a courtyard.

Fitzhugh said, apologetically, "Sorry it's such a mess. I often sleep here when work prevents my going home."

"That's okay," Marius murmured, sure there wasn't any other home but not very interested. Poverty and its shifts were no novelty to him. "Where's this teapot of yours?"

There were two other doors. Fitzhugh opened one, revealing a large closet, almost a small room, with shelves along one wall. He brought out a cardboard box which he set down carefully on the table. From it, he lifted something enveloped in layers of tissue paper. He unwrapped it gingerly, as if he expected it to explode.

Marius drew close. As the last of the paper came off, he raised his eyebrows.

A delicate pale blue glaze of the type called *ying ch'ing,* or shadowy blue, and a gourd-shaped body with a slender curved spout and a long handle: a wine pot—the spout had misled Fitzhugh—perhaps showing some Mongolian influence and perhaps early Yüan rather than Sung. Not the best he had ever seen, but very good indeed. He took it away from Fitzhugh, his fingers, better than his eyes, delighting in the shape and texture.

"Very nice," he said, with his usual restraint, and turning it over to look at the bottom, froze. The pot came from the Beauvoir Collection.

Marius looked speculatively at that tall, thin, haggard man, at his clean, square-fingered hands and threadbare cuffs. Competent and poor, once in the army, used to decision, now living from hand to mouth in an office which could not even afford a secretary. It must have taken plenty of nerve and ability to steal the wine pot. The Beauvoir Collection had its own little building in Bloomsbury Square, reasonably secure and well guarded. It had also taken a certain background to choose a piece like this. Fitzhugh had probably served in the East.

Marius regarded him with respect. It had been a good story, well played out. Anyone could find out George Bright's name, of course, and that minor weakness didn't count for much. If only Fitzhugh had been a little more careful it might have worked, for Marius had no doubt he'd never have passed up a piece of this quality.

And now what? Obviously, the best thing was to get away as quickly as possible and call the cops. At the same time, he hated to let Fitzhugh out of his sight. Suppose the man's suspicions were aroused, suppose he were to buzz off with the pot and vanish into the anthill?

Fitzhugh was watching him expectantly. Marius said, "Yes, well, I think it's right. Hard to tell from a casual inspection. It's hard to say whether it's been repaired, too." He said it with some notion of getting the other to let him take the pot with him, but realized that that would never work. Then, all at once, he had a better idea.

Fitzhugh was saying, "How old did you say it was?"

"I haven't said, yet. But if you want to sell it—you *do* want to sell it, don't you?"

"Oh, yes, of course."

THE CHINA EXPERT

"Okay, well, I'd have to be certain there weren't any flaws in it, no carefully covered-up repairs."

"If you mean you'd like to take it away, I'm afraid I can't allow that."

"It won't be necessary. All I have to do is look at it under ultraviolet light. And as it happens, I have a viewer with me."

"A viewer?"

"Yes, lots of dealers carry them. A portable device. The only thing is, I need complete darkness."

Marius opened his briefcase. He had with him a little battery-powered combination flashlight and magnifying glass, a gadget he found useful now and then when the light was poor. "Here we are," he said, cheerfully.

"That?"

"That's right, that's all it is. It won't take a minute. Let's see, you haven't any heavy curtains in here, just Venetian blinds. That's no good. What about your closet?"

"You mean go into the closet?"

"Yes, sure, it looked big enough for both of us to get into. It won't take a minute. I'll just check the pot over and make sure there aren't any hidden cracks."

As he spoke, he handed the pot to Fitzhugh so the man wouldn't think he was preparing to run off with it. Then he opened the door of the closet and politely motioned the other to precede him. The instant Fitzhugh was inside, he slammed the door. He had seen that it had a key, and he turned it. It was all beautifully simple, both pot and thief neatly stored together.

"Open up, damn you!" Fitzhugh was shouting, rattling the doorknob.

"Don't drop that pot," Marius said, turning the key a little so it wouldn't be shaken out of the lock.

There was a phone on the bookcase. He lifted it. Instead of a dial tone, somebody said, "Yes?"

Obviously, a party line. "Sorry," Marius said. "Would you mind getting off? I want to call the police."

"Not at all," said the other and hung up.

Marius waited for the dial tone. He was still waiting when the door to the outer office opened and two men strode in. One of them pinioned his arms, the other unlocked the closet.

Fitzhugh came out, red in the face, still holding the pot, and stared at Marius.

"Done!" he said, bitterly. "And by a bloody amateur."

Chapter 2

Marius stopped struggling. The man who had been holding him let him go but stood nearby. He was making an odd noise which Marius suddenly identified as a chuckle.

Fitzhugh said, "All right, why don't you two push off?" He watched them leave, and when the door was shut, shook his head. "I'm sorry about all this, Mr. Kagan," he said. "Something went wrong and I'm not sure what it was. However, please sit down. I'll explain everything."

In spite of his confusion, Marius had sense enough left to see the change in Fitzhugh. It was no more than a subtle shading, something crisper in his manner, a touch more firmness in his posture. The difference was, Marius decided, that now he would have stood out in a crowd instead of vanishing.

It was obvious, too, from his tone and what he said, that he was not what he had seemed. From all his years as a highly competitive dealer, Marius had learned the value of patience and restraint, which he balanced against his natural pugnacity and heat. He sat down without a word.

Fitzhugh put the wine pot on the table, gently, and sat down opposite Marius. He had controlled his look of annoyance and he made himself smile.

"I've worked it out," he said. "You thought I was a criminal. You thought I'd stolen that thing. Right?"

"Well, what are you?" Marius said.

"I'm a member of the Security Service."

"Security? You mean espionage?"

"That's right, Mr. Kagan. Actually, counterespionage."

"You're kidding," Marius said, automatically.

"I'm afraid not. Quite serious."

Marius began to laugh. "You think I'm a spy? Me? You must be out of your mind."

"No, sir. I know quite well you're not a spy."

"I don't get it, then. What was all this horseshit about your wanting to sell that pot? How did you get hold of it? How could you—?"

Fitzhugh raised a hand. "I told you I'd explain everything." He took out a case and extracted from it a long brown cheroot. "Do you smoke? No? Very wise. It's a frightfully expensive vice, these days." He lit the cheroot carefully and sat back. "Of course, you know about the opening of the Museum of the East?"

"The Adjai? Certainly. I had planned to come back from Paris next week for the preview. I have an invitation."

It would have been odd if he hadn't. The Museum of the East, newly constructed on a piece of ground near Lambeth Bridge on the South Bank, was to be devoted exclusively to the art of China, Japan, India, and the smaller countries of Southeast Asia. It was an artistic coup for Britain as well as a political one. Its exhibits were to be painting, drawing, and sculpture; no ethnographical or craft materials were to be included, with one exception on which almost every authority agreed—the exquisite porcelain and pottery of a thousand years of Chinese history, which were acknowledged to be admissible to the ranks of art.

Another equally good reason for their inclusion was that the museum owed its existence in the first place to King Ibrahim Adjai of Rasulullah, whose oil revenues amounted to a large share of the Arab capital invested with the Bank of England, and who was an ardent collector of Chinese porcelain.

The king had been educated at Oxford, where he had made his mark as a fast left-handed bowler and connoisseur of malt whiskies. However, he had wandered into the Ashmolean one day and had there become enchanted by an exhibition of nineteenth-century famille rose; from that it was only a step to excursions up to London to visit the Victoria and Albert and the Percival David Collection. He had begun collecting himself under the firm guidance of Aram Tashjian of Brook Street, and by the time he was forty had a collection almost unequaled in private hands.

At about this time, the idea of the museum had been proposed to him, half-jokingly, by Tashjian. He had said, one day, that wealth was the handmaiden of culture, and that the names of rich men were best remembered for their intelligent accumulation of art from the time of the Medici to that of Widener, Duveen, and Frick. Wasn't it time, he said, that the fortune of an Arab magnate was put to the same purpose? Why not perpetuate the name of Ibrahim Adjai by attaching it to a repository which would rival that of the Jewish merchant Hirshhorn, in Washington?

With those words, the conversation had become more serious. Other people were drawn in for consultation. The eminent authority John Vallier, who had written extensively on Oriental painting and prints, made a strong case for a museum of art rather than one devoted to porcelain alone. For instance, he said, although fine examples of Chinese art were scattered as far apart as Cleveland and Stockholm, you might wander through the major museums—the Louvre, the Tate, the Metropolitan—without ever discovering that a whole body of important painting existed representing five hundred years of art from one of the world's oldest and greatest cultures. "Look in the Tate!" he cried, "You'll see a great many pictures by Matisse, Degas, Whistler, and Cassatt, but not one single painting by any of the Japanese masters who so profoundly influenced them! It's not only a deprivation, it is an insult."

Tashjian agreed, and added that one must also be practical: public exposure increased the value of art. Housing the Adjai collection in a museum of international stature would make it even more valuable. King Ibrahim nodded, only remarking drily that he failed to see how the prices of good porcelain could be any higher than they already were.

In the end, he determined to go ahead with the project. He decided on London for several reasons. He saw it as the center of the West. Furthermore, it contained a considerable part of his investments.

At the time, détente between the Soviet Union and the United States had, in a way, shut out China, which saw itself as the third great power in the world. A museum of this sort, small as the gesture might be, paved the road for a new and more important bond of attachment between the United Kingdom and China which might lead to an increased economic tie between them and even open the way for connections between China and the European Community. The minor Asian nations, too, who were in one way or another dependent on China, would benefit. Britain's position, clearly established as taking the lead to bring China into the West, could only be strengthened, a fact which the government at that time was quick to recognize, especially as King Ibrahim would put up three-quarters of the price for the construction and maintenance of the museum. Nor was the king greedy. The establishment would be called The Museum of the East, with no more than a modest bronze plaque paying tribute to the generosity of Ibrahim Muhammad Adjai Ibn Hassan. It was, however, almost from the first generally referred to as the Adjai, a fact which gave Aram Tashjian as much satisfaction as the king since he had paid the costs of a public relations firm to assure just that result.

The formal opening of the building had been set for July 7, a good time for tourists. On the day before that, there would be a preview for specialists and for the press. Marius, an old friend and competitor of Tashjian's, had been among the first invited.

He said to Fitzhugh, "I don't see what spies have to do with the opening of the museum. Or what that has to do with me."

"Perhaps you will, Mr. Kagan." Fitzhugh examined the end of his cheroot and added, in a somber tone, "There may not be an opening."

"What?"

"The Sung vase has disappeared."

The Sung vase. Marius sat up. Although the Adjai contained a number of vases from the three-hundred-year span of that dynasty, he knew exactly what Fitzhugh meant. For the opening, each of the countries represented had loaned one of its national treasures. China, to mark its gratification, had sent a vase of great but simple beauty, bearing a brief inscription in the "gold brocade" calligraphy of the Emperor Hui Tsung himself. Examples of his handwriting in the style he had invented were rare enough, but to find one on a piece of porcelain was unique; however, Hui Tsung had been noted for his conviviality, and it was assumed that this inscription marked a gift to some friend, or a game or jest. Although the beauty of the vase would have made it valuable enough, with this addition its worth could hardly be computed.

"Disappeared?" Marius repeated. "What do you mean? Lost?"

"Worse than that," said Fitzhugh. "It's been stolen."

He stubbed out his cheroot, almost angrily, and went on, "A lot of care was put into the operation of getting it over here. The Chinese sent their own team, four men from their Special Branch and a curator from Peking to carry it—"

"Kao Chun."

"Yes. When he got here a couple of days ago, he went to the building, was received by the director, and at once put the vase into the special case which had been prepared for it by the Chinese government and for which only he had the keys. The Chinese wouldn't allow anyone else to touch it or handle it. They said politely—and with some justice—that they didn't want their hosts to bear so great a responsibility."

"I can understand that. It does look like going a little too far, but I guess they're like that."

"Well, day before yesterday, in broad daylight, the vase was taken," Fitzhugh said, heavily.

"Good Christ!" Marius threw himself back in his chair. "What kind of complicated snatch did they pull? What'd they do, come in through the ceiling?"

"No," Fitzhugh replied. "I really don't think I'm at liberty to tell you."

Marius rubbed his chin, pinched it up between finger and thumb, regarding Fitzhugh meditatively. "Listen," he said. "I'm not stupid, you know. I get the feeling you're in some kind of trouble, and for some reason you need my help."

"So?"

"Very simple. You've dragged me over here and put me through all this nonsense about appraising a pot that doesn't belong to you, you've changed your tune and told me you're a secret agent—I don't have any way of knowing whether you're lying or not. Have I?"

"I'm afraid I haven't any identity card, if that's what you mean, Mr. Kagan," said Fitzhugh, with a pinched smile. "You'll just have to take my word for it. But you're right, I do want something from you."

"Okay. Then suppose you start by opening up a little. How was the vase stolen? Let's say my profession makes me curious."

Fitzhugh nodded. "All right. I'll tell you what happened, but I want your promise that you won't talk about it."

"Sure."

Fitzhugh fixed his eyes on Marius's. They were small, deep-set among wrinkles, pale blue, and cold. "In the first place, you haven't been in the museum yet, have you? Well, it's square and two-storied. Exhibition halls run all round its ground floor, connected by a corridor. Inside, there's another square, the inner hall, which is used for loan or special exhibitions. That's where the vase was. The inner hall has two doors, front and back, giving out on the corridor. Upstairs, there are the director's office and some more exhibition rooms. Then, in back, there's a one-story wing housing the Adjai Collection. The basement is for storage, workrooms, all the rest of it.

"The building has its own guards, of course, but the Metropolitan Police had also detailed men to watch the place before the opening. And one of the Chinese Special Branch people was always on duty in the inner hall. They took it in shifts, round the clock.

"The case itself was a double one, with two hinged panels with a lock on each. There was also an electrical alarm system which was triggered if the locks were forced or the glass broken. We weren't really anticipating any trouble, you know. It's not the sort of thing a thief would try for—nothing he could do with it if he did steal it. Still, we took more than ordinary precautions. However, they weren't enough."

"Then how—?" Marius began, with visions in his head of films he had seen: crooks dressed in black, shooting ropes from building to building, and so on.

"It was very simple," Fitzhugh said. "The thief just walked in and took it. You see, everyone had thought about a gang breaking into the building, or cracking the case, but they'd forgotten all about the real weak point, which was somewhere else. The keys."

"You mean Kao Chun!"

"That's right. He was staying at the Chinese Embassy, but he wasn't going about under guard or anything like that. Yesterday morning, he took a stroll in Kensington Gardens. You know how people tend to lie about on the grass in weather like this? He was found lying under a tree, quite peacefully. Hadn't been noticed for hours."

"Dead?"

"Oh, no. He'd been given a shot of something. He was asleep."

"And the keys—?"

"I'm coming to that. In the museum, it had been a busy morning. The last exhibits were being hung, the floors were being polished, people were bustling in and out, and everyone who came in was carefully checked. All except one. The dustman.

"There was a lot of rubbish to be picked up, packing materials, papers, that sort of thing. They had contracted with a small company in Camden Town to collect it, and what looked like the company's lorry drove round to the back and a couple of men began work. The guard barely paid any attention to them; they might have been invisible.

"What seems to have happened was that one of them, under cover of the work, walked into the basement. A few minutes later, he strolled into the inner hall through the rear door. He was then wearing a white dust coat like a laboratory technician. He went purposefully to the case, unlocked it, took out the vase, and walked off with it."

"Just like that?"

"Just like that. Nobody stopped him because he was so calm and self-assured that everyone thought he was authorized to take it. He even smiled and nodded at the guard, who glanced at him and then went back to watching the front entrance to the hall. That was all there was to it. Presumably, he went downstairs and joined his chums, who had finished loading the dust cart by then, and they all drove off. It wasn't until Geoffrey Foster, the director, came through the inner hall and noticed the empty case that they began to realize they'd been diddled."

Marius began laughing. "I'm sorry," he said. "It's just the thought of that fellow marching in so calmly—"

"I know," said Fitzhugh. "Everyone behaved foolishly. Patterns of thought, you know. We try not to, but we all tend to think in certain patterns. You put something valuable into a safe and you're so busy making the lock strong that you forget how weak the back may be. People *do* do utterly stupid things."

Marius remembered Tom Bridger leaving a briefcase full of money in a New York taxi and nodded.

"Yes," he said, "but suppose Kao Chun hadn't gone out for a walk that morning?"

"Oh, I daresay whoever managed the job kept him under surveillance. There was no reason for him to remain locked up in the embassy once he'd delivered the vase. They knew he'd go out sooner or later, and I imagine if he had had a guard with him, they'd have had some plan for dealing with the situation."

Fitzhugh interlaced his fingers and stared at them. "Now, of course, things are sticky," he said. "The eyes of the world, you might say, are going to be turned on that museum on July seventh. The Chinese ambassador will be there, and so will the Prime Minister and the ambassadors of the other countries. It's become a political matter. We shall look jolly silly if we can't even guard a little vase properly, and so will the Chinese. They don't like losing face and neither do we. It may put paid to the whole thing."

"Who took it?" said Marius. "The Russians?"

"We have several leads," Fitzhugh answered, curtly.

"Okay, next question. What do you want from me? I'll be glad to do what I can, but I'm no cop."

"It's quite simple, Mr. Kagan. I got your name from Dr. Bright, as an expert in this Chinese ware. I want you to identify the vase for me when I find it."

Marius blinked. "Why? Don't you have any pictures of it?"

"Oh, yes." Fitzhugh dug into an inside pocket of his jacket and brought out a glossy photo which he tossed over to Marius. Marius had seen the vase in the papers but the pictures were never clear enough. This was a fine, sharp color shot and he examined it carefully.

Fitzhugh said, "Would you say that was a fairly common shape?"

"The shape? Oh, yes, not unusual."

"And it's a sort of pale blue?"

"Well, there are blues and blues. This is a type of glaze called *ch'ing pai,* not exactly white but—"

"Yes, yes, never mind that. Suppose someone offered me a Chinese vase of this shape and color with some scribbles painted on the side of it, I wouldn't know whether it was a fake or a copy or what. Whereas, when I showed you this pot—" He tapped the wine jar which stood between them, and went on, "You knew it was good even though you had to examine it with your ultraviolet gadget. You never did say how old it was, though."

"Sorry about that," Marius grinned. "My ultraviolet gadget is only a flashlight. Just a way of getting you into that closet. As for this, it's a wine pot, dating from somewhere around the latter part of the thirteenth century."

"That's right, that's what they said it was. There you are, then. I intend to find this thing but it's possible somebody may offer me a substitute. You'll be my insurance."

Marius thought about that. "I don't know," he said, at last. "I'm pretty busy. How long do you think it will take?"

"I can't say. But I can tell you this," Fitzhugh said, gravely, leaning forward across the table, "it's damned important. I know how busy you are. I've done a bit of homework on you, Mr. Kagan. I know you are planning to go to Sussex tomorrow to look at some Chinese bronzes. Then, you'll be seeing Mr. Sun, and on Friday a collector named Nicholas Conran. You're booked on the eleven o'clock flight to Paris on Saturday. Shall I go on?"

"No, that's enough," Marius said, feeling strangely queasy. It made him speak more sharply than he had intended. "You're pretty nosy, aren't you?"

"I have to be. I'm not in this for the thrill of it. The diplomatic association between Britain and China is at stake, and perhaps the future of a lot of people in one way or another. You may lose money by staying here instead of going to Paris, but I can't help that. I hope you'll see this is more important than money."

Marius flinched. He knew perfectly well what was in the other's mind, the implied contempt, the oblique slur —not so oblique sometimes—*Jews and their money.*

Well, there was just this much truth in it, that in a highly competitive profession like his, in which the balance between success and catastrophe was so precarious, in which you depended only on your wits and the stakes might be so large, one could not help being calculating. Tom Bridger was no different, nor was Sun Wei. But in fact, it wasn't the thought of profit that was holding Marius back, now. It was really that the whole situation was so improbable: spies, international politics, so much hanging on the whereabouts of a piece of porcelain, the kind of object he thought of as his everyday bread and butter suddenly turning into a piece in a harsh game different from anything he had ever been involved in.

He said, stiffly, "It's not a question of money. Suppose you don't turn this damn thing up for two or three months? What am I supposed to do—go out of business just to give your country a hand? It really hasn't got anything to do with me, you know."

"I understand," Fitzhugh said, in a placatory tone. "It can't take a couple of months, however. If we haven't found it by the sixth, we'll be in trouble. We're keeping the theft a secret now, but by the time of the preview we'll have to say something. After that, it won't matter any longer."

"Why not? Don't you want to get it back after that date?"

"You see, Mr. Kagan, we feel fairly certain the piece was stolen for political reasons. Not all of us feel that, but I do and so does my chief. That is, the object of the theft was to discredit Britain and put a spoke in the wheel of this effort to promote friendship between East and West. Well, if we don't turn up the piece by the preview, the object of the people who've stolen it will have been achieved. They'll probably return it. They don't want it, you see."

Marius nodded. He was beginning to feel hemmed in, as he might by a persistent customer who was hard to satisfy. "But look, I'm not English. There are at least a dozen people over here, your own people, who could identify this vase for you. What about Foster, the director of the museum?"

"You don't seem to have been listening, Mr. Kagan. Sorry, I don't mean to be short with you. I'm rather tired." Fitzhugh passed a hand over his face. "We've been hard at it for the past two days. Look here, this isn't going to be a picnic. It'll be dangerous. I can't try to conceal that from you. I'd thought you might see it for yourself, once you understood the political nature of the crime. Just think about the English experts for a moment. Foster has a bad heart. Tashjian is in his early eighties. Beltane is seventy. Penelope Wyndham and Angela Lowery—well, I can't ask women. Bright has four children.

Sun must be twenty years older than you, and he's a fat man—"

"Okay, okay. I'm the young, athletic one, the one who can dodge faster than the others, is that it?"

"And you haven't any ties. Also, if you don't mind my saying so, you're a foreigner. They—whoever they are who organized the job—won't associate you with us. Therefore, they won't try to knock you out of the affair."

He paused, and Marius pondered that phrase for a moment, with a slight chill.

"Or at any rate," Fitzhugh went on, "that's what I'm hoping."

"That's what I'm hoping, too," Marius said, drily. He shrugged. And then, looking into himself, he discovered that the chill of apprehension had become something else, a tingle of anticipation. Was it possible he could actually be looking forward to danger, trouble, being mixed up in a crime of these dimensions?

Possible, he told himself, with odd elation.

"All right," he said, aloud. "God knows why, but I'll do it. Me, a man who's always loved peace and quiet."

Fitzhugh said, "Splendid. I'm very relieved. Now, you're at the Comus, aren't you? Well, just go on about your affairs and when I need you I'll get word to you. We've got nine days. If you haven't heard from me at all by next Friday morning—ah, but I hope you will. Can you cancel your Paris plans without arousing any particular attention?"

"Yes, that'll be easy enough."

Fitzhugh ran his little finger over his toothbrush moustache, a curiously foppish gesture in him. He picked another cheroot out of his case. He had lost some of his air of authority and was looking haggard, again.

"I *am* tired," he said. "One more thing. You just might hear something useful. After all, it's possible the vase was stolen by an ordinary thief—or I should say, an extraordinary one—and since it's in your field . . . well, one never knows. You might even be approached by someone who wants to get rid of it. I'd better give you a phone number where you can reach me, or leave a message."

He took out a worn, shabby wallet and found a card which read, *Electrodyne Research Co., Ltd., Manchester–London,* and in one corner, *Patrick Fitzhugh.* There was a London telephone number in the other corner. Fitzhugh passed the card to Marius.

"If you ring me," he said, "dial that number backward. In other words, instead of 629–5426, you dial 624–5926. Got that?"

"What would happen if I dialed it the other way? The phone would explode?"

Fitzhugh smiled without amusement. "You'd get the 'engaged' signal."

There was just enough intrigue in this to delight Marius. He put the card away and said, "Great. So now I'm an international spy. How did you ever get into this business?"

"Oh, like any civil servant," Fitzhugh replied, vaguely. "By the way, there's one thing I'm curious about. Why did you become suspicious? I mean, what made you think I had stolen that teapot or whatever it is?"

Marius picked up the wine pot and turned it upside down to show the tiny round sticker bearing the initials *PB* and a number, pasted on the bottom. "That's the label of the Beauvoir Collection. I suppose you got them to loan you the pot so you could test me, is that it?"

"Yes. It wasn't easy, but I was able to persuade Metcalfe that a good deal hung on it, without actually telling him why."

Simon Metcalfe was the curator of the Beauvoir, and

an acquaintance of Marius's. For a fleeting instant, remembering what Fitzhugh had said, Marius wondered why Metcalfe wouldn't have been a better choice. He was single, an avid golfer, younger than Marius, and probably in better shape.

But Fitzhugh was saying, "I didn't even know collectors put labels on their things. I never looked at the bottom and wouldn't have noticed it if I had. It shows you, doesn't it? One little slip—" He uttered a short bark of a laugh. "I shall hope that whoever stole the Sung vase will make his little slip. Everyone does, sooner or later."

He stood up. "That's all clear, then, is it?" He held out a hand and Marius got up, too, and shook it. "Thank you very much. And remember, keep this to yourself, will you?"

"Relax," Marius said. "I understand. After all," he added with a straight face, "we're in the same business, now."

Chapter 3

When he emerged from the building housing Electrodyne Research and Edible Gold Crosses, Marius glanced at his watch. He was astonished to find it was only a little after one. It felt as though he had been inside for days. He wasn't very hungry and walked to a nearby pub he knew, where he could get a pint of bitter and a sandwich and where, undisturbed, he could turn over in his head what had happened.

Most of all, he was conscious of that strange lightness of spirits which had not left him. Once, long ago, he had taken a sea trip and early one morning had seen dolphins swimming alongside the ship. For some days, there had been only the steel-colored sea, a tumbled waste, too vast even to be hostile; now, all at once, the sight of those sleek dark backs plunging and rising joyously by twos and threes had changed his vision, and he saw that the great sweep of water was a living meadow in which they gamboled. His heart had lifted at the sight, the same sensation he felt now.

And he knew why. He had begun to feel empty. It could not be said he didn't enjoy his work, but the edge was off things. What had once given him great enjoyment now gave him only mild pleasure; it seemed he had no time for anything else. He was too busy, dashing from place to place, inspecting, making decisions to buy, to sell, to trade. And the worst of it was that his stock was beauty. Those elegant porcelains, those powerful bronzes, those deceptively simple paintings, had become mere objects with which he could consolidate his position in the world. Was it not the painter Chu Ta who had driven away people who wanted to buy his works, but had given them away free to those who loved them but couldn't pay? Once Marius had felt a kind of kinship with such a painter. Nowadays he would have thought him mad, if he thought about it at all.

Take this morning. He had enjoyed the victory over Claudel and the neatness with which he had disposed of the screen he didn't want, while also clearing his debt to Nakamura. But he had forgotten the screen itself; he couldn't even remember what was painted on it. And his victory had been so trivial! A revenge for a pinprick, amounting to a kick in the pants, all of it governed by small malice and ending nowhere. He had a capacity in him for larger, deeper emotions but he filled it with pettiness. He was like a talented musician with twenty years of training who spent his time tuning pianos. Nor was it only his work. He enjoyed his food and drink, but it seemed to him that his mealtimes were passed in business discussions, so that he often couldn't tell whether he was drinking a vintage claret or water. Nor was sex much different, nothing more than a way of passing a little time. Without a deeper involvement with another person, it became no more than casual pleasure, a relief for the body's urgent need but as soon forgotten as taken on.

You had to let things go before you could really appreciate them, he told himself, thinking of Mei. I suppose it's only when you can give something up freely that you see it for what it is. A stab of unhappiness went through him and he turned his mind away from the memory.

But now, Fitzhugh had come along with his story of theft and intrigue, and his proposal, and things had changed. Not much, but enough to put a little color into life. He, Marius, knew something hidden from the world in general, and he was on the inside, taking an active part in it. And there was the spice of danger, as well, making a challenge to which he had to respond. Ever since he had been a kid, being short, being a Jew, had made it impossible for him to avoid a dare.

He finished his sandwich and washed down the slightly stale bread with beer, wondering why the English persisted in selling what they called "fresh cut sandwiches," which meant they had been made early that morning and lined up for several hours in a case to be ready for lunch. An odd custom. He began to think about the theft. Fitzhugh had asked him to keep his ears open, but of course he had promised not to talk to anyone about it. It occurred to him, however, that the people at the museum knew about it, and they included his friend Geoffrey Foster, the director. Surely, his promise to Fitzhugh couldn't include those already in the know? Several questions were already rising in his mind—he was incapable of not playing the detective, out of the same impulse that made him want to try to read a painter's signature, or find the provenance of a bronze. For instance, that man who had so coolly walked in and taken the vase, was he Chinese or Caucasian? How had the thieves known what kind of garbage truck to use, and how could they have taken the chance that the real contractor's truck wouldn't turn up at the same time? But no doubt Fitzhugh, or the police, or whoever was in charge, had already asked the same questions and were looking for the answers.

He had a vision of the thief, strolling unconcernedly into the exhibition hall, nodding to the guards, calmly unlocking the case and walking off with the vase. Involuntarily, he laughed, and embarrassed, turned it into a cough. He was sitting at a small table in a corner and nobody had paid any attention to him. Almost nobody, he amended, as his eyes met those of a man standing at the bar who at once looked away.

It was enough, at any rate, to make him finish his drink and leave. Outside, the sun seemed hotter than ever. The windows were as bright as mirrors, and the air above the pavement shimmered. The beer he had had began sweating through his shirt. He had no appointments until two-thirty and he felt restless. He began walking towards Brook Street, drawn in the direction of Tashjian's gallery although he had nothing to do there until next morning when he was to see Aram on business before catching the train to Brighton.

His mind returned to Fitzhugh's proposition, not that it had ever been very far from it. He felt again the slight puzzlement over why he had been chosen. Why not Simon Metcalfe, after all, who also met all the qualifications? "You're a foreigner," Fitzhugh had said, and something about being knocked out of the affair. He had a vision of going with Fitzhugh to some dark and squalid den where, as he examined the vase, someone crept up behind him with a knife. "You must take this seriously," Fitzhugh had said. Maybe he really wasn't taking it seriously enough.

He stopped to look into the window of an art gallery, the sight of a Rouault cleansing his palate, so to speak. Superimposed on the paintings, he saw the reflection of the street behind him. Across the street, just that moment lighting a cigarette, stood the man who had been looking at him in the pub.

There was no mistaking him, a round, slightly bulging forehead, an owl's beak of a nose. It couldn't be coincidence that he had come all this way to stop and light a cigarette when Marius stopped.

They're on to me already! Marius thought, not without a thrill of excitement. He looked ostentatiously at his watch and then, with the air of a man who has just discovered that he is late for an appointment, began walking again but more rapidly. He turned left into Davies Street and strode purposefully along, going as fast as he could, but when he turned the corner into Berkeley Square he ran as fast as he could, to the left, where there was a tiny lane north of the square. Ducking behind a jutting flight of stairs, he peeped out and saw his pursuer come into view. The man looked about, and then made his way across the street to the railings of the square.

Marius did not wait to watch. He darted into the lane which led to a long alleyway called Bourdon Street, which he had in the past used as a shortcut to Sotheby's. Along Bourdon Street, its curve concealing him, under the iron balconies of a low block of flats, and round another corner where the alley divided, one arm going to Grosvenor Street, the other under a kind of tunnel into New Bond Street. He chose the tunnel, hoping there would be a taxi cruising down to the Westbury Hotel where there were always Americans. He was in luck. One appeared as if on cue and he hopped into it.

"Turn left down there at Conduit Street, will you?" he panted. "And just keep going until I catch my breath."

He couldn't help feeling smug. Not only had he shaken off the tail, he had demonstrated that he knew his London, a kind of childish pleasure at being so at home in a foreign city. The same thing made Tom Bridger boast, "I'm as much of a New Yorker as you are when I'm there." He looked at his watch, this time in earnest, and saw he had plenty of time to get to his appointment.

He gave the driver the address and settled back to enjoy the ride, and to decide how best to persuade James Pike-Gorham not to put the lovely *chang yao* vase into the sale room but instead to sell it to *him.*

Thus happily absorbed, he got out of the cab on Chesham Street and paid the driver. He started for the house. His way was blocked, and he found himself staring at the man he had so successfully evaded.

"How—?" Marius began.

"That's all right, sir," the fellow said. "I didn't bother, you see. Mr. Fitzhugh gave me your schedule in case I lost you, so I just took a cab and came here."

"Mr. Fitzhugh? You're one of his men?"

"Well, I work with him, sir. Now don't go doing that again, please. I'm watching you for your own protection, see?"

"Oh," said Marius. "I see. Okay. Thanks."

He was so put out, however, that he lost the *chang yao* vase.

•

Chapter 4

When the door had closed on the American dealer, Patrick Fitzhugh still stood for a time staring at it, his goodbye smile slowly freezing into something very like a snarl. He didn't like Americans, he didn't like Jews, he didn't like Commander Wilde to whom he had been seconded in this case from D.I.5, and he didn't particularly like himself. That was always the problem, that feeling of shuddering tension which ended in self-hatred when you played a double game. Well, there was a palliative for it. He pulled open the top drawer of the mahogany bureau and took out the bottle.

There were still a couple of inches left. He didn't bother with a glass but unscrewed the top and held it greedily to his lips.

He felt better when he put it away, but not much. The way he had been trapped in the closet still rankled, but he flattered himself that he had been able to throttle his annoyance. He had handled the dwarfish little sod very smoothly, after all. Nevertheless, he got the bottle out again and took another sip or two.

He had good reason to drink. For two decades he had been living on a tightrope.

He had been twenty when he was commissioned, fresh, daring, ready for anything, having distinguished himself during the last thrust into Germany. Almost as the war ended, he had been made a lieutenant. It had been a foot on the ladder, and for the next two years life had been full of heady promise. He got along well with people, had an engaging, lively manner without being thrusting, and in spite of his youth was a good listener. He was quick with languages, too, and while busy with rehabilitation work with DPs on the edge of the Russian Zone, had added Russian to the German he already spoke reasonably well.

But there were strains, mainly that of living up to his rank as an officer and a gentleman. Things might have been different in another sort of regiment, but his was the 26th Hussars, fashionable enough to satisfy a taste for upper-class life, but difficult for a young subaltern with very little money. His mess bill and his debts increased as his resources dwindled, and eventually he allowed himself to be led into shady dealings, including a black market operation in medical supplies, especially drugs.

It was at this stage that he was approached by the Russians. They foresaw a use for him, and they had two persuasive arguments: blackmail and reward. One of their agents had been involved in Lübeck with the drug ring, and they knew all about Fitzhugh. They threatened to expose him; on the other hand, if he would be cooperative there would be some money it, not much but enough to satisfy his creditors. It wasn't much they wanted in return, only for him to pass some information along to British Security. It would be a simple job. He would pretend to have learned, from one of the displaced persons he dealt with, the name of a Russian agent in a key position. He had little choice but to agree.

The agent was one who had made himself expendable by untrustworthy behavior, and so could be sacrificed, for the Russians had a longer range operation in view. Just as they had hoped, Fitzhugh made a good impression on the Security man he talked to by his zeal, his intelligence, the value of the information and his quickness in passing it along, and also by his ability to speak both Russian and German. It occurred to Security that they could use such a man. Fitzhugh's background was good —a respectable but decayed middle-class family, an equally respectable school, no taint of awkward political leanings, young enough to be molded. He was given several assignments which he carried out satisfactorily. He heard nothing further from the Russians and tried to tell himself that they had finished with him. When at last he returned to London, Security persuaded him to leave the army, and a place was found for him in what was then called M.I.5.

For ten years, he applied himself to whatever he was given, acquiring a reputation for being hardworking, a good chap but a bit dim, perhaps a little too reticent. The truth was, he was afraid to push himself forward, never wholly forgetting the slip that lay in his past. And then the Russians contacted him again, reminding him that they had never really let him go. He was one of their keys, fitting neatly into a receptacle in the heart of the enemy camp. He was trapped.

It has been said that the serviceable life of a spy is about seven years, but by now Fitzhugh had tripled that without being discovered. The cost had been terrible: steady fear, the fear of being found out, the fear of being abandoned by his other employers, the uncertainty of any sort of future, and above all, the constant loneliness. He had survived. He had survived mainly because neither side had so far called on him for any major operation. He remained useful without becoming important. His camouflage had been to be second-rate, dependable but not brilliant, a cloak of darkness which kept him in action without calling attention to him.

All at once, however, things had become more difficult. The theft of the Sung vase and his assignment to work with Commander Wilde, the police officer in charge of the case, had put him in a delicate position. Enough to drive anyone to drink, but he had had a twenty-year head start.

He put the bottle away for the second time and looked into the other office. The two leg men were still there, they had not yet gone into their own office which was behind the filing cabinet.

He said, "You saw him off all right? Good. Thomas, you go after him. Here's his schedule of appointments. I want to know everyone who contacts him from now on."

The man with the beaky nose took off. The other said, "Do you still need me?"

"Not just now," said Fitzhugh. "Go have some lunch. Just clear my line, first, please."

He knew perfectly well he'd be hearing from Wilde before long.

But it was Guy Neuville who called him first.

"Can I speak to the managing director of Electrodyne Research, please?"

"What do you want, Guy?"

"This is Herr Direktor Krauss of International Fiddles."

"Stop playing about. What is it?"

"What, don't you enjoy my careful attempts at secrecy?"

"Look, I'm busy." He never knew, with Guy, whether it was the whim of the moment that made him jocular, or the fact that he was trying to conceal some disaster. Every call, therefore, provided its own terrors. "Come to the point, will you?"

"Don't get shirty, Patrick. Are you alone? I'm just round the corner. I'm coming up."

"I'd rather you didn't," Fitzhugh began, but the other had rung off.

They had met five or six years before, when Fitzhugh had been instructed by his Russian case officer to contact Neuville, then a bright electronics expert in his early thirties. He was extravagant and flamboyant, a member of a landed family, moving between Mayfair society and rock circles; also, he made no secret of his sympathy for radical causes. He was involved in highly sensitive research and it was felt an advance to him might be profitable. He and Fitzhugh had taken to each other in spite of the difference in their ages. His extroversion seemed to set off Fitzhugh's reserve. Neuville found the older man a good listener and a good foil; Fitzhugh enjoyed his un-self-conscious frivolity. Besides, there was an element of snobbishness on Fitzhugh's part. Neuville belonged to the gentry, and Fitzhugh had never forgotten that he had once been an officer in a smart regiment. Eventually, the open approach was made and Neuville had come in. He had passed across certain valuable information, for which he had been well paid. But as time went on, he became more unstable, more unpredictable. His work had suffered, and as he lost jobs he lost his usefulness to Fitzhugh's masters. By now, he was becoming hard to put up with.

When he came in, Fitzhugh sighed, knowing there would be trouble. His eyes were bloodshot and glassy, and as he shook hands the faint waft of hash came from him.

"I'd be grateful if you didn't stare at me in that distinctly hostile way," he said.

"I'm not. I don't like that stuff you smoke," Fitzhugh said, sourly.

"You're a frightful puritan, Pat. Good title for a book, that. Puritan Pat, Boy Spy." He tittered. "But it was the best *kif*—I mean, the best butter, don't I? *Kif* for two."

"Look, I'm expecting someone to phone," Fitzhugh said. "I don't want to seem inhospitable, but will you come to the point? I suppose there was some reason you wanted to see me."

"You suppose right," Neuville said. He made his way to the armchair and sat down, rather heavily, and for a time said nothing else.

Fitzhugh regarded him with distaste. His long hair was lusterless and there was dandruff on the collar of his leather jacket. He had a tangled beard, and his white turtleneck was not quite clean. He wore a string of Tibetan prayer beads around his neck, and he played with them with one hand while with the other he drummed and drummed lightly on the arm of the chair. His cheeks were pendulous, his complexion waxy, and his once slender and dapper figure had become flabby.

How can someone grow old so rapidly? Fitzhugh asked himself. He can't be more than thirty-eight. But I know the answer to that one, it is not so much dissipation as fear.

Neuville said, at last, "I've picked up some more information about that new computer, the IC354."

"Is that all?"

"It's terribly exciting."

"Not to me."

"Not worth anything at all?"

"I told you, Guy, we're not interested. And I don't want you coming here like this. It won't do."

"I was afraid you'd say that." He suddenly stopped drumming and clasped his left hand around the fingers of his right to hold them still. "All right, Pat. I've been approached by that Chinese fellow again, the same one. And this time, I think I'm going to talk to him. I really must have something to go on with. A couple of free meals in a Chinese restaurant are better than nothing."

Fitzhugh felt himself grow heavy. For something to do to ease the tension he pulled out his case and lighted a cheroot. They were among his few extravagances, Mahawats, from Fox's, and he tried to limit his quantity but this had been, and looked like going on being, a trying day.

He said, through the smoke, "You're a fool, Guy. You can't trust them."

"Well, whom can I trust? Nobody but you. That's why I'm telling you all this. I mean, I haven't any real friends left. Can I trust your people?"

"But the Chinese will use you and then drop you. My people won't like it, and you'll be caught between the two, a nut in the nutcrackers. I won't be able to help you."

He felt some concern for Guy, but not much. Chiefly, he was thinking, If he begins talking to the Chinese it's only a matter of time before they find out about me.

Guy said, "Look here, Pat. You don't seem to get the picture. I'm desperate, see? Things are very heavy. If I can't get anything from the Russians, I'll have to deal with anyone I can. To coin a phrase, beggars can't be choosers, can they?"

Fitzhugh forced sympathy into his voice. "Don't you think I understand? I know exactly how difficult it is for you. I'm only thinking of your welfare. What does this chap want from you?"

Guy put on his injured look. "Well, really, I don't

know that I ought to tell even you. I simply can't afford that sort of generosity. You see that, don't you?"

Fitzhugh sighed. "Yes, I see," he said. "How much do you want?"

"Do you mean for that question, or for my information about the IC354?"

"Both."

"Let's not bargain, it's so undignified. Say a couple of hundred."

Before Fitzhugh could reply, the telephone rang. Although he had been expecting it, he jumped.

"Do you mind?" he said. "Go into the other office. I'll be with you again in a minute."

He waited until the door was shut before answering the phone.

"Fitzhugh? Wilde here."

"Yes, Commander," he said.

"Can we talk?"

Automatically, he glanced at the office door. "Yes."

"You had a chap with you this morning, short fellow, looks slightly Oriental. I want to know about him."

"Oh, yes, I was going to tell you about him this afternoon. He's an American, actually, an art dealer."

"What's his name?"

"Marius Kagan. He specializes in Chinese things. That's his cover."

"What do you mean, his cover?"

"He's a CIA man," Fitzhugh said, smoothly. "Has some contacts on the other side, and I thought he'd be helpful. I've put him in the picture."

"You've told him about the burglary? Damn it, Fitzhugh, I don't want to have anything to do with those people," said Wilde.

"I'm sorry, Commander, but I'm trying to do what I can."

Wilde grunted. He had a particularly annoying grunt, into which he managed to inject skepticism and derision.

"I know you're not convinced this is a political case," Fitzhugh went on. "But after all, I was attached to you because—"

"All right. Just stay in line. And after this, you'd better talk to me before going off half-cocked."

"Certainly, sir," Fitzhugh said, keeping a fine line between hurt dignity and earnestness. "I'm sorry."

"Luckily, it's not that important. At least I hope not. Not this time," Wilde added, as an afterthought, and hung up.

Fitzhugh let out his breath. Wilde had bought it. Now, he thought, let's hope other people buy it, as well. So far, so good. He went to the door and called Neuville in.

"Now, then, Guy," he said. "I can't settle this sort of thing on my own. I haven't got two hundred pounds, or I'd give it to you myself, right now, just to get you off the hook. I shall have to talk it over with—" He gave a jerk of his head, meaning *them.* "I'll do my best to convince them that that rubbish about the computer is worth the money. I won't say anything about the Chinese. You can understand why, I hope?"

"I suppose you mean they'll be jealous," Neuville said, sulkily. "How long shall I have to wait? Good God, Pat, if you only knew how lousy it is to have to keep putting people off. I mean, they're following me around in the streets now, pulling at my sleeve. I'll take to mugging pretty soon."

"Be patient. It won't take long. I'll get in touch with you in a day or so."

"I'll ring you here."

"No. I'll get in touch with *you.*" He put a hand on Neuville's shoulder, pressing it with his fingers affectionately. "Do as I say, Guy. I'm on your side. You know that, don't you? Try to hold out. Be patient."

"Yes, all right." Neuville moved away, and then turned back. "Can you let me have a fiver, meanwhile?" he said with hollow jauntiness.

Fitzhugh gave him a note and saw him off, watching him go down the stairs almost as if he were falling from step to step.

He had no intention whatever of discussing the matter with Sergeyev. He knew perfectly well what that one would say: "Your own fault, shows bad judgment, *Feetzgu.*" It would end with their keeping a sharper eye on *him*. No, he would have to decide on his own what to do about Guy. He shut the door slowly, noiselessly, thoughtfully.

Chapter 5

In the Comus's high-ceilinged, paneled dining room, Marius finished his breakfast and opened the *Times* with a little tremor of anticipation. There was, however, nothing about the theft of the vase. Only the usual fare served up like the inevitable bacon and eggs of an English breakfast: a threatened strike which might paralyze industry, a raid by Palestinian guerrillas, four more dead in Belfast explosions, an air crash, death, violence, ruin, tolling from the pages which were being turned so peacefully by dozens of eaters all over the comfortable room.

They had, then, managed to keep the story under wraps. They must have appealed to the newspapers, or threatened them—there was, Marius knew, some kind of Official Secrets Act which could be invoked to prevent the publication of anything that might be contrary to the national interest, and this might well qualify. On the front page there was a picture of the Chinese ambassador, Wang I-chang, shaking hands with the Prime Minister, both faces, the round and the thin, toothily split: "A new era of cordiality and mutual cooperation is thus heralded which shall surmount . . ." and so on. Marius thought of what Fitzhugh had said. "We shall look jolly silly if we can't guard a little vase properly, and so will the Chinese." There, if you liked, was a typical British understatement. They would look like blundering, incompetent mountebanks which, he reflected, as he finished his coffee, would probably describe all the governments in the world anyway.

He left, folding up his paper, listening to the chatter, the American voices sounding oddly flat and nasal after so much British speech: "That Charlie is a real beautiful human being." "So the net of it is, I told him, Johnny baby, I said . . ." A tall, slender woman with shining lacquered hair and a jaw like a prizefighter waved brightly at Marius as he passed and said, "Hi, there! Going sightseeing today?" Their acquaintance dated from traveling up and down in the lift together. He muffled his fury and gave her a tight smile.

As usual, he had to face the bland stupidity certain kinds of English employees are trained to display. Phoning to cancel his Paris flight, he was told politely that the flight was fully booked and there were no more seats, and the more he tried to make himself understood, the oftener he was told the same thing, until, foaming with rage, he slammed down the receiver, determined to go to the airline and kill the clerk there. Instead, he gave his ticket to the hall porter with a pound and told him either to get it canceled or go to Paris, whichever he preferred.

Feeling a little better, he got his briefcase and went out. The weather was back to normal, a sky like a sheet of lead and a thin, damp wind tinged with burned gasoline. There was a giant American car which seemed to be called a Sabretooth parked across the street from the hotel, and Marius mused on the curious fact that American cars are usually named after beasts of prey or weapons, while English cars are called Sunbeam or Princess. Things will look up in Britain, he thought, when they start calling their cars Cut, Smash, or Crunch. A man with a clean-cut advertising face, a little cleft in his chin like Cary Grant, and sunglasses came out of the hotel behind him and as he passed Marius, glanced at him and said in a strangely mumbling voice, as if through badly fitting dentures, "Hi, how are you?" "Almost over my leprosy," Marius replied amiably, heading for Brook Street.

Aram Tashjian was a kind of fixture in the world of Oriental art. Nobody could remember when he hadn't been around, and King Ibrahim was by no means the only connoisseur he had nursed from youth to maturity. There was hardly a collection in the world which did not owe some of its best pieces to him. He sat in the dingy back office, inaccessible to all except a few favored customers, while his two young assistants, both over forty, dealt with the generality of visitors in the fine, large outer gallery.

Marius was shown in without delay, and Tashjian rose to shake hands, saying, "How are you, my boy?"

"You're good for my ego, Aram. You make me feel like a kid."

"You *are* a kid. When I was your age, I had already lost two fortunes in two wars. Would you like some coffee?"

He pressed a button and said, "Bring a pot of coffee, Dora, my dear."

He had an ageless look. Fine wrinkles netted the surface of his face, hardly discernible in this light, but his eyes were bright and lively and his dark hair, Marius noted with envy, showed no signs of thinning. With his hooked nose and pointed chin he looked like a benevolent Mr. Punch, but Marius knew well that he could be a ruthless opponent.

This morning, at any rate, they weren't in competition. They had joined forces to buy the contents of an estate with the understanding that Tashjian would get the Chün stoneware and Marius the bronze vessels, and all that remained was to settle the details of payment and shipping and to decide between them how to dispose of the things neither wanted. This occupied the best part of an agreeable hour.

At the end of that time, as they were chatting, Marius said, cautiously, "And how are things going at the Adjai?"

"As well as can be expected. Very busy, with less than a fortnight to the preview."

"You've been over there every day, I suppose?" It had occurred to Marius that any promise not to talk about the theft couldn't apply to Tashjian, who must certainly know about it if anyone did; perhaps he could find out something more.

"Oh, yes. Purely as an observer, of course. I don't want to have Geoffrey thinking I am interfering with him. A fine man."

"Can't be beat. I heard some funny rumors, though."

Tashjian's eyebrows rose. "About him?"

"No, no, about the opening. Some sort of trouble—something being lost or stolen."

He met the other's eyes. Competent professionals that they were, they understood each other immediately.

The old man smiled. "It's hard to keep secrets in this business. How did you find out?"

"I can't tell you, Aram. I'd like to, but I have to protect my sources."

"It was Sun Chih-mo, no doubt. And I've been led to believe the Chinese were close-mouthed."

Marius blinked, but then recollected that Sun had been acting as an advisor to Foster for late seventeenth- and eighteenth-century painting, on which he was an authority, and so might well have been at the museum on the day of the robbery.

Without assenting, he simply said, "It was a big shock. As I got it, a man just walked in and took the thing. Were you there, then?"

"I was upstairs with Geoffrey. We came down together, talking, and walked through the inner hall. You haven't seen the place, there is a big hall, a kind of atrium, where we're showing the special loans. We walked straight past the case in which we had the Sung vase and suddenly Geoffrey stopped—what do Americans call it when you look at something twice?"

"A double take."

"Yes, exactly." Tashjian beamed, repeating the interesting foreign phrase, "A double take. That is what he did. So did I. I couldn't believe it. I said, 'Where is it?' He said, 'That's what I'd like to know.' Then the confusion began."

"I can imagine. The thing I can't understand is—I hear there was a Chinese Secret Service man right there in the hall all the time. How come he never got suspicious?"

Tashjian picked up a carved ivory seal and turned it over between his short, knotted fingers, smoothing its surfaces lovingly. "Let me ask you, my boy, you're a sharp young fellow, what kind of picture do you have in your mind of the sort of chap who would steal an important object like that?"

Marius said, doubtfully, "I hadn't really thought—well, I guess he'd have to be—I don't know. If I were casting the part for a movie, I'd say Paul Newman. Do you know him?"

"I don't go to the cinema very often, but I think I know what you mean. Youngish looking but mature, dashing, rather tough, eh? Well, from the description of the two people who noticed him at all, the Chinese and an attendant who was unpacking a case, the thief was gray-haired and wore glasses."

"Really? Was he a Westerner?"

"No. We later heard from the policeman in charge of the case, Commander Wilde, that the Secret Service man said he looked like a scholar, very quiet, and a Cantonese."

"That's interesting," Marius said. "And I'm told he was wearing a white smock over his clothes, as if he'd been working at restoration. But didn't the guard down in the basement notice him? Surely he'd have noticed a gray-haired garbage man with glasses?"

Tashjian chuckled. "He didn't. Perhaps the man was wearing a cap. I know what I should have done if I had been the thief, I'd have worn a gray wig and a pair of spectacles with plain glass. I'd have had my white smock folded up under my jacket."

"And when he left through the basement, carrying the vase—?"

"If he was smart, he had some sort of carrier, a holster you might say, under the jacket, too. He would slip the vase into it. After all, it isn't very large, you know. Or, there were boxes of rubbish down there, he might have put the vase into one of them and walked out carrying it that way."

Marius shook his head. "Incredible. What about that garbage truck—I mean, the dust cart? They were taking a chance that the real one wouldn't turn up, weren't they?"

"Not that day, no. Looking it up, Geoffrey found that they were not supposed to come until the next day."

"Somebody must have known that."

"I suppose so," said Tashjian. "We can't imagine who.

So far as we know, the museum staff are all perfectly loyal. Which of them would have been mixed up in such a thing?"

He shrugged again, answering himself. "For money, people will do anything. The police are—what is that word—*grilling* them. And investigating their background." He dropped his voice. "You know what is being said? That it is the Russians who were behind it."

"Yes, I know. They're the ones who stand to gain most by it, aren't they? I mean, in terms of embarrassing the Chinese and the British."

"Maybe so. There are others, of course."

"I can't believe it would have been an ordinary thief. Where would he sell it?"

"Oh, there's always a buyer for everything. You've been in the trade long enough to know that. But I was thinking of the Formosans. They would like very much to have the Reds made to look fools. And to make trouble when Britain and China seem to be cooperating with each other, eh?"

"That's true. You think the thief may have been a Formosan?"

Tashjian closed his eyes, turning down the corners of his mouth expressively. "Who knows? The Russians, too, have Chinese-looking people in their nation."

"What about those garbagemen?" Marius asked, struck by a thought. "Were they Chinese as well?"

"Oh, no, Westerners. One Chinese dustman, but not a whole crew. The police are looking for them. I don't think they are going to find them so easily. This was a clever job, my boy." He croaked with amusement. "Very clever. Almost as clever as if it had been done by an Armenian."

Marius laughed with him. "I wouldn't put it past you,

you old crook, to steal the vase and sell it back to the Chinese. You'd need a gray wig, too. How do you manage to keep looking so young?"

"A clear conscience, my boy," said Tashjian, who had only the day before unloaded an extremely dubious Han tomb figurine on an unsuspecting German dealer. "I never have anything to reproach myself with."

Marius left in ample time to get to his Brighton train. He had plenty to think about on the trip down. He wondered if far too much was being made of the political nature of the theft. After all, what better cover could an art thief have than to have everyone chasing around looking for Russian or Formosan spies? A fine piece of ceramics, like a fine painting, was currency anywhere where there were collectors, and by now it might be on its way to almost any corner of the earth, to be hidden away and enjoyed in secret. Marius had known collectors who had had no scruples whatever, who would cheerfully have swindled their best friends out of a good piece, who had willingly paid out bribes to smuggle things past uncooperative Customs officers, and who wouldn't mind in the least scoring off any government in the world for the sake of a prize. Nor were there many clues to go on, as far as he could see. Well, in any case it was really none of his business, he told himself, but even with the thought he had to smile, remembering that when he got on the train he had caught a glimpse of a familiar figure, the man with the bulging forehead and little curved nose, getting on, too, at the other end of the coach. It *was* his business, whether he liked it or not.

Considerably more his business was the appraisal of the bronzes in Brighton, most of them of good enough quality to make the work enjoyable. It took up most of the afternoon, and he rang Paul Li in London to be sure their dinner date was still on. "Bring along the Chu Ta you got the other day," Li said. "I would like very much to look at it again, before you sell it to someone richer than I am."

"That'd be hard to find, Paul," Marius said. "You're rich enough. I'll see you at seven."

He had hoped they'd meet early because a Chinese dinner, especially in Paul's own restaurant, was certain to go on for a good long time. Nor was he disappointed; by eight-thirty they had only arrived at the steamed mullet.

Li Piao—he had anglicized it into Paul—stood somewhat outside the various segments of the Chinese community in London. He came from a well-to-do family but had never shown any particular sympathy for the exiles in Taiwan. On the other hand, neither had he openly expressed any attachment to the People's Republic. He had little in common with the lower-class people in the catering trade and even had difficulty speaking Cantonese to those he hired. Nor did he seem to have many connections with the wealthier refugees from Hong Kong, although he kept up perfectly friendly relations with many of them. There was something aloof, almost aristocratic, about him. His English was flawless, and he seemed to have plenty of money which came from no one knew where, although Mei had once hinted to Marius that he had secret backing from the People's Republic and that his restaurant was used as a listening post. Whether this was the case or not, he ran it as a kind of hobby, being mainly concerned, it appeared, with buying ceramics, jade, an occasional good painting, and snuff bottles, some of which he kept and some sold to his many rich friends abroad. He was good-looking in a donnish sort of way, affecting thick-rimmed glasses and English tweeds. It was impossible to tell his age.

He poured another glass of wine for Marius, who said, *"Hsieh-hsieh, go lah."*

Li chuckled. "It always surprises me to hear you speak Chinese. You learned it from a Northerner, but where? Had you been to China?"

"No, I acquired it thanks to the United States Army. I was drafted in forty-four, when I was just a kid, and they sent me to school to learn it. The reason for that is kind of complicated, in fact. I came from a little town called Pratts Falls, near Rochester. We had a rich man living there, Mr. Jardin, who had traveled all over the East, and I did some odd jobs for him. He kind of took to me, and it was in his house that I first saw some Chinese ceramics. I fell for them right off. I decided that when I was older, I was going to own stuff like that for myself."

He reached with his chopsticks for another piece of fish, smiling at the memory, and said, "I was a tough kid, you know. Once I set my mind on something I'd kill myself rather than give it up. Anyway, Mr. Jardin taught me what he knew, which wasn't much, and also taught me a few words of Chinese. So when I was drafted and they asked me if I spoke any other languages, I boastfully said, yes, Chinese. I trotted out my ten words or so, and it must have impressed them; anyway, they sent me to school to learn some more. There was a lot of talk about cooperation with the Chinese in those days—the Burma Road and the whole campaign against the Japanese on the mainland, you know—and they figured I'd be an interpreter. I was in school for almost a year. Then, I don't know if you know how the army does things, but it must be the same everywhere, when I got out they sent me to France as a replacement in an infantry outfit."

Li laughed. "That sounds reasonable. And did you fight in Europe?"

"I never fought anywhere. I never fired a shot. I spent the next three weeks or so as a clerk in Headquarters and then the war was over. I can't say I was sorry."

"It was lucky you kept up your knowledge of the language. You speak quite well."

"Thanks, but I know my limitations. Anyway, it helped get me into this business. When I got back to the States, the first thing I did was make a list of all the dealers in New York who handled Oriental antiques. Then I went around from one to another asking for a job. I didn't know much—Mr. Jardin's pieces had mostly been nineteenth-century painted pieces—but I got a job with a man named Rosen because I had two qualifications, I was Jewish and I spoke Chinese."

He picked up his wineglass and looked meditatively into it. "My God, that was thirty years ago, Paul. It gives me a shiver when I think of it. *Kan pei.*" He upended the glass. "You must have been a little kid, then."

Li returned the toast, and said, "Don't bank on it. I am nearly your age. And don't forget that in China we count as the first birthday the day you are born, so I have an extra year."

He glanced at the waiter who swooped away the fish, while another brought a plate of beef with hot bean curd and chili.

"Where were you during the war?" Marius asked, feeling bold enough for so personal a question since they had been speaking so intimately.

Li said, "In Shanghai. My grandfather had a large house there. My father was an army officer. It was my grandfather who saw that I was educated and who developed my taste for art. He was an official, one of the old-fashioned sort, an amateur painter and calligrapher with quite a reputation. I still own several of his paintings in the style of Tung Ch'i-ch'ang, whom he venerated. In fact—this will amuse you—some years ago I was offered one of his paintings by a Hong Kong dealer who tried to pass it off as a genuine Tung Ch'i-ch'ang."

Marius nodded without surprise. Because of the long tradition in Chinese painting of copying or working "in the style of—" the ranks of Chinese art were swelled by forgeries, and even experts were often hard put to it to declare the authenticity of a picture.

"His calligraphy," Li went on, "is excellent. I must show you some one day. Very strong and upright, the man himself."

He leaned back, pushing his glasses up on his nose with a finger. "I have never lost the ambition which I got from him, to retire some day to a quiet place in the country, to give up all this—" he waved a hand vaguely around him, meaning the world of business, "to paint, to compose poetry, to write elegantly and meet with friends. 'My kitchen shares the mountain green,'" he finished, quoting from an ancient poem.

"The ideal of the gentlemen painters," said Marius. "Not a bad life, either. But where the hell can anyone go nowadays, where the mountain green won't be full of oil slick, or the kitchen loaded with radioactivity? And if you went back to China and tried it, they'd put you to work on a collective farm."

Li nodded. "I don't say they are right, but the new things in the world are calling for new measures," he said. "Perhaps just because of what you mention, the pollution and so on, it is too late for any of us to retire and indulge ourselves. We are living on the edge of a great change, Marius. A time when the Western ideal of individualism may be—"

He broke off, as a shadow fell across the table. Two

men stood there, a Chinese with a rather hard, closed face, and a Westerner, a trifle behind him. Marius thought, at first, that the Westerner was dressed oddly for an old man, but looking again saw that he must be in his late thirties, although his face was puffy and sagging. He had a rather scruffy beard and long hair that fell about the collar of his dark leather jacket. Instead of a tie, he wore a string of beads over a Mexican linen shirt.

The Chinese said rapidly, in his own language, "Sorry to interrupt, but I want to talk to this foreigner in private, and the waiter—"

Li cut in sharply, and in English, "It's a pleasure to see you. Allow me to present my friend, Marius Kagan, an American visitor. Marius, this is Mr. Ch'in, an old acquaintance."

The other bowed as Marius rose, and gave a smile that was like a crack opening in cement. He said, in heavily accented English, "Great pleasure meet you, sir. You forgive me I talk Mr. Li and interrupt you."

"Of course," said Marius. "I understand. Don't mind me."

"I think I know what Mr. Ch'in wants," Li said. "He always prefers a table in the back room, and it must be rather crowded there. However, for a friend, I'm sure we can make room."

As he called to the waiter, the bearded man said, "Mr. Kagan, is it? Haven't we met before? You're a dealer in Oriental art, aren't you?"

"That's right. But I'm sorry, I don't remember you."

"Neuville. Guy Neuville. I'm sure we've seen each other somewhere. I'm interested in Far Eastern art."

"Is that so? Are you a collector?"

Neuville laughed, looking suddenly boyish. "All I can afford to collect now are memories of what nice things look like. And bills, of course; my collection of unpaid bills is probably the finest in London. But I love those marvelous figures they are continually finding in tombs—horses, little dancers, that sort of thing."

In spite of his appearance, he somehow managed to retain a certain charm, as if the shadow of an ebullient youth still clung about him. He added, with a touch of wistfulness, "I don't suppose you'd have some little thing in the lowest sort of price range?"

"Well, not much, I'm afraid—"

"No, I thought not."

He seemed so mortified at having even asked, that Marius said quickly, "But maybe I could find something. Why don't you give me a ring? I'm at the Comus. You can generally catch me there in the morning, before about nine-thirty."

"How kind of you," Neuville said, brightening. "I shall certainly take advantage of it. I'll ring you in a day or so."

"Do that," said Marius. He felt a momentary misgiving, but after all, a customer was a customer, and Neuville's accent was cultured and his jacket was clearly expensive.

When the two had gone, escorted by a waiter, Li said, "I'd be careful of that man, if I were you."

"Do you know him?"

"I know his type. He's a sponger."

"Maybe. But I've had customers before who started out by saying they were broke and ended up spending a thousand dollars."

"Don't say I haven't warned you," said Li.

His tone was so somber that Marius looked at him. He smiled, shook his head and said with a change of manner, "I'm afraid this dish is cold. You like chicken livers, don't you? We're going to have *ho yo jun-gon,* and some chicken with yellow bean sauce."

Marius was pursuing the last bit of chicken, reminding himself ruefully that he had heard ivory chopsticks called "the Nimble Brothers," when Li nodded, greeting someone who had just entered the restaurant, and saying, in Chinese, "Good to see you again. Are you all alone?"

"I am meeting some friends. They will be here soon."

At that voice, Marius felt a surge of blood to his head. His ears began ringing and for an instant, although he could see Li's lips moving, he could hear nothing. He turned in his chair.

"Hello, Mei," was what he intended to say, but no sound came out.

Her cheeks grew rosy as she stared at him, and she covered her mouth with her hand.

"You pardon me," she said, in English. "I go sit down, wait for my friends."

Marius watched her go to a table in a far corner. She ordered a drink—he knew exactly what it would be, manzanilla, and she would drink very little of it for she had no head for alcohol. She had seated herself so that she could watch the door, and she had her profile to him but resolutely did not turn her head. The light gilded the smooth outline of her short nose, the round firm chin, the delicate curve of her mouth. He turned away, biting his lip, and held out his glass to Li, regardless of manners.

Li began to talk about the problems he was having with his chef, carefully not mentioning her, while Marius ate and drank in silence. But he was aware of her there, a dozen yards away, as if she were breathing down his neck.

Ridiculous! he said to himself. I don't want to talk to her, I haven't anything to say, we'd be polite and casual as if we were a pair of strangers. And at the same time, below the level of those thoughts, he was trying to find some way of approaching her, of hearing her voice again even if she said nothing but hello and good-bye.

At last, breaking into what Li was saying without being aware that he was doing so, he said, "Paul, wouldn't you like to see the Chu Ta painting? I've brought it along, as you asked."

Li said, with surprise, "Why, yes. I thought we'd go upstairs after dinner and have some brandy in my office."

"Why wait? Let's hang it up right here. It's a tiny little picture. We can hang it on the bottom of that light fixture and look at it while we finish."

Li's face was politely expressionless. "If you like," he said. "But not on the fixture, it's too high."

He called a waiter and told him to get a drawing pin from the order board in the kitchen. When the man came back with it, Li stuck it into the wall near the table while Marius opened his briefcase, took out the scroll, and unrolled it. The painting itself, set in a fine old mount, was the size of a sheet of typewriter paper, but because of its power seemed larger. Done with all the vigor of that eccentric artist, it showed a gentleman walking in contemplation beneath a towering mountain peak, a common enough subject but given immense grandeur by Chu Ta's brush. Marius hung it up, and they sat back to admire it.

"Ah, that's the real thing," Li murmured.

"Oh, yes, I haven't much doubt of it," said Marius. "I know where it came from, too, although they didn't mention it in the catalogue. It's from the Ogushi Collection, originally."

"Look there, at the pines, done with such strength. *Yu p'o li.*" The phrase referred not only to the power of the painting, but to an inner spiritual power of the artist himself.

All Marius's senses were stretched. It was as if he had extruded a dozen antennae so that he could feel Mei approaching, he knew when she was standing behind him. He had known that the sight of this painting would fetch her.

"Chu Ta," she whispered, so softly that he felt it rather than heard it.

He turned. "It's lovely, isn't it?"

She nodded, not looking at him.

"Sit down," he said, pulling out a chair.

"Yes, please do," said Li. He regarded them with amusement and benevolence, having understood why Marius had been so suddenly insistent on showing the picture.

Mei hesitated and then sat. Her elbow brushed Marius, and he shivered, all his desire awakening, all the past forgotten. A faint, spicy scent came from her.

He moved closer and said, softly, "I've missed you."

"Don't say it," she murmured.

"Why not? Do you expect me to believe you haven't been thinking of me? I know better. Tom Bridger told me."

"Oh." She lifted her chin and smiled, tiny dimples appearing high on her cheekbones, under the eyes. "All right, then you know I want know all about you. I'm sorry. I should not have done."

"Yes, you should," Marius said, angrily. "Jesus, how I've missed you! I've thought of you every minute, all this time. And it's been worse here in London, knowing you were somewhere and not seeing you." He clasped his hand around hers. "Come on, let's get the hell out of here."

"But my friends—"

"Oh, screw your friends. Never mind them. Paul will tell them you got sick or something."

He rose, dragging her up with him. Li said, "Are you going?"

"That's right. When Mei's friends come, tell them she was kidnapped by a foreign devil."

"But we haven't finished eating," Li protested, mischievously.

"I'm sorry, Paul. I haven't any more appetite."

"Here! Just a minute! You're forgetting the painting. Now I know," he went on, as Marius quickly rolled it up and thrust it into his briefcase, "that you are really hopeless. 'Hold back the river with your hand sooner than a man in love.'"

"Yeah, very good," Marius grunted, snapping the locks. "You people have a saying for everything."

"No, I just made that up," Li said.

Marius hurried Mei into the street. He held her arm as if he thought she might escape, but she walked docilely beside him to Shaftesbury Avenue, where they caught a cab.

"Where are we going?" she said.

"I'm at the Comus. Too public. We'll go to your place."

She said nothing as he gave the driver her address. All the way there, he held her hand in silence. He began to feel that he had acted too impetuously; it was not regret but nervousness.

Mei had a compact but comfortable flat in a new building north of the Bayswater Road, three good-sized rooms with large windows that faced southward, high enough to overlook the dark mass of the park with its walks picked out in strings of lamps. There was even a tiny balcony, and when she had opened the french doors a damp, leafy, summery waft filled the room. She snapped on a couple of lamps, then took off her light jacket and stood facing Marius.

"I know you like drink something," she said. "I make you whisky with ice."

"All right."

He watched as she got ice from the kitchen and opened her little cupboard-bar. Even in so simple an act as this she displayed a lissome grace, every movement executed as if part of some ritual dance. She brought the glass to him, and stood before him as he sipped it, with something expectant in her smile.

"You're a great whisky pourer," he said.

"I wait for you say that."

He put the glass down and she was in his arms.

They understood each other. There was none of the blind urgency of youth, but a calmer, deeper passion in which each knew the other's need, responded to the other's rhythm. His arm about her waist, her head against his shoulder, they went to the bedroom; without hurry, they undressed; smiling, they sought each other.

Later, Marius said, "You are lovelier than ever." He spoke in Chinese, knowing that his accent amused her.

"You are still a great flatterer. I am an ugly old woman. But it pleases me. You haven't changed."

"Don't speak so rapidly." He kissed her heavy-lidded eyes, tasting the dew of sweat that lay on her cheeks. "I'm getting up. I want to finish that drink."

She got up as well, and slid open the closet door. "Some of your things are still here. I have kept them to —to remind me—" She shook her head.

She gave him his robe, Japanese dark-red silk, and herself put on a dressing gown. "Are you hungry?" she asked.

"I could nosh a little something," he said in English.

She said, critically, her head on one side, "I think you make love to me only to get an appetite."

He caught her close, the thin silk between them emphasizing the curves of her body. "I could eat you," he said. "But all I want's a sandwich."

They sat close together on the couch, taking alternate bites of the sandwich of Ardennes pâté—typically, she had taken the trouble to cut off the crusts. Marius said, "I haven't even asked you anything about yourself."

"Nothing has changed. My business is doing well, but people are going crazy. This—" she made a circle of her thumb and forefinger, for money, "is all they think of, and as it loses its value they become like animals. But I still manage. Richard"—that was her son—"is working on his thesis. He has been busy. Oh, there's nothing to say. And you? Have you been well?"

He nodded, gazing around the room at the remembered things, the curious combination of junk and exquisite works of art, the jumble of her taste between East and West: a hideous Victorian clock, a seventeenth-century cloisonné incense burner, an Art Nouveau desk, dreadful lampshades with bobbles, a couple of richly patinated Chinese chairs. Among the paintings on the walls, all by Chinese masters, was a mounted fan on which, in soft, melting ink, was sketched a magpie in flight and beside it a poem in the characteristic powerful, slanting calligraphy of Wu Ch'ang-shih.

"That's new," Marius said.

"It refers to the Bird Bridge. You know the story?"

"I think so. But you tell me, anyway."

"It is about Chih Lu, the Sky Weaver. She was one of the seven daughters of the Kitchen God, and once, when she was bathing in a stream, she was seen by a young farmer who was filled with desire for her. He stole her clothes—"

"A good way to get to meet a girl. I must try it."

She pushed his hand away. "Listen. She came naked to him to ask for her clothes and he made love to her. They lived happily together for three years, but then the gods became angry because she was no longer weaving for them. They forced her to return to the star where she lived. When the Cowherd died he became an immortal and was given a star of his own. But the Queen of Heaven drew her hairpin across the sky and made the Milky Way which separated his star from that of the Weaver. Now they can meet only once a year, when all the magpies of the world make the Bird Bridge with their wings. But if clouds cover the sky, the bridge cannot be made and we see their tears fall as rain."

"Lovely," Marius said, lightly. Then, all at once, he understood, for her eyes were brimming. He slipped an arm about her.

"We're going to work something out," he said. "I don't know what, but something. Even if it has to be only once a year—"

She broke away from him and went to the balcony. She stood looking out at the night, hugging her dressing gown about her although the air was mild. Then, with an impatient gesture, she shut the french windows, and turned to him.

"I don't want to talk about it," she said. "It is hopeless. Let us see each other now, that's enough. While you are in London, all right, but we won't think about what comes afterward. How long have we? How long will you be here?"

"I don't know," Marius said, remembering what Fitzhugh had told him. "Maybe a week. Not longer than the seventh or eighth of July."

"Then we have until then. I don't want to look any further."

"No," he said. "Maybe not."

Maybe it was better not to plan but to live in the present. To take what you could get and be grateful for it. That way, too, there was no responsibility. He sighed.

"Come back to bed," he said.

Deep dark; a faint, damp breeze stirring the gauze curtain. Mei sat up, listening to Marius's regular breathing. She lit the tiny spark of the pocket flashlight she kept on the bedside table and looked at the clock. It was past three. She moved the light, looking at his dark hair, the edge of his cheekbone, his nose buried like a child's in the pillow.

It was because she loved him that this meeting had been so painful. Well, she had tried to warn him. But what good was a warning when she herself had wanted so desperately to see him again?

Carefully, she got out of bed, pulling on her robe. She stood for a moment to be sure there was no alteration in his breathing, and then went into the living room, softly closing the door behind her. She took up the phone and dialed a number.

"Ni shih shai?—Who's that?" said a sleepy voice.

"Yuan Mei, here. Everything went as you planned. He's here now."

"Good. Has he said anything about the vase?"

"Not yet."

"You must find out what he knows. And don't forget his hotel room. There may be something—notes, a record of telephone calls—"

She sighed heavily. "I wish there were someone else," she said, knowing what the answer would be.

"Don't be a fool. You are the best person, the one he

cannot suspect. Don't play games. There isn't that much time."

He hung up. She sat on for a long time, in the dark, and the words she had spoken earlier that evening went on echoing in her head: *tears like rain, tears fell like rain.*

Chapter 6

The rain poured down, and Marius, hatless, coatless, umbrellaless, stood on the corner near Mei's apartment house smiling largely on the world. He stood with one hand raised but he had forgotten about it, so that when a taxi pulled up it surprised him.

"Good morning," he said to the driver. "Lovely day, isn't it? The Comus Hotel, please."

People don't appreciate how beautiful this weather is, he told himself. The streets glistened, reflecting the swift bodies of cars. The rain fell in fragments of crystal, and along the eaves of the taxi, above the windows, hung rows of drops, clear and shining. Everything glowed pallidly under the dove-colored sky, punctuated by the golden lights of shop windows and the polished black of umbrellas. Marius beamed at everything, the placards of news vendors: SIEGE OF GUNMAN CONTINUES IN FIFTH DAY, 4 DEAD IN STREET BATTLE, and a large yellow and black sign erected by the Automobile Association at Marble Arch saying, DEMONSTRATION—AVOID THIS AREA ON JUNE 30TH.

He was going to see Mei again at five. She would cook dinner, just as she used to, and they would have a cozy, quiet evening. The nagging problems which he knew were just ahead, the same question about how they were to go on, the doubts of the future, all that could be postponed; what mattered was that they were together again, and that he felt lighthearted and alive.

At the hotel there were several messages. Among the calls from customers was a note from Guy Neuville asking if he could stop by sometime; with an effort, Marius remembered him as the man in the leather jacket whom he had met in Li's restaurant. He had left a number. After he had changed and sent his wet clothes to the valet, Marius called it. Neuville sounded as if he were talking in his sleep, but seemed to wake up when he understood who Marius was and agreed to come at nine-thirty the following morning. That, Marius figured, would allow time for him to be brushed off, if necessary, without cutting into the day too deeply.

He made a few other calls, lined up his appointments for the rest of the day, and set out. The rain was slackening, and a faint yellow gleam was beginning to show itself above the buildings. In front of the hotel a man stood looking through a London atlas, the *A to Z*. He wore a tweed hat and a raincoat and, incongruously, sunglasses. He nodded to Marius, who said good morning automatically, trying to think where he had seen that cleft chin and those sunglasses before. But he was distracted from the attempt by the appearance, from one of the phone booths across the street, of the man Fitzhugh had sent to follow him. Marius smiled and waved, but the other, who looked soggy, simply hunched his shoulders and jammed his hands deeper into the pockets of his mackintosh.

At three, Marius was at the small but stylish gallery in Grosvenor Street, on the door of which, in chaste gold letters, was printed *"C. M. Sun, Works of Art,"* and in the window a single spotlighted jade bowl.

Sun had been one of those rich people who, correctly

foreseeing the course of history, had been able to move quietly out of the way before the victory of the People's Republic. He had taken over the family business when his father, a prominent art dealer, had died in the late 1920s and had been astute enough to preserve his treasures through the unrest and war of the next two decades. In 1947, he had begun to convert his possessions into gold ingots which he had smuggled to Hong Kong, and from there, some years later, he had moved to Britain. He was now approaching the lucky age of seventy-one, with the prominent belly and smooth complexion of one who has lived according to the Precepts and has been suitably rewarded with at least four of the Five Blessings.

He was also rather old-fashioned in his ways, and Marius enjoyed doing business with him. It meant sitting over cups of tea, gossip, and the leisurely inspection of paintings or hardstone carvings, which were Sun's specialties. Today was no exception; they had been half an hour in chat and had only then come round to the real point of Marius's visit, a soft, rich landscape by Huang P'ing-hung. As in so much Chinese art, the question of authenticity was a vexing one, since forging and copying had a long, respectable history in that country. However, Marius had pretty much satisfied himself that not only were the signature and seals impeccable, but the brush was indeed that of Huang.

Sun remarked, "There is another one, very much like but I think not so good, which you will see it when Adjai opens."

Marius glanced at him, recalling what Tashjian had said.

"*If* it opens," he replied, on impulse.

Sun blinked, and then smiled, folding his hands across

his paunch. "Oh," he said. "That's right, you saw Aram Tashjian yesterday. I thought Armenians had special reputation for keep quiet."

He so exactly echoed Tashjian's words that Marius burst out laughing. "Don't blame him," he said. "Word does get around, you know. You were there when it happened, weren't you?"

"Oh, yes, I was in upstairs gallery. I heard the commotion and went to see what's going on. They were running about like chickens."

"And the vase was gone, eh? What happened then?"

"Then the police come, great fuss, we all questioned, but there was nothing to tell. Do you know how it was stolen?"

Marius nodded. "It must have been a beautiful piece," he said, wistfully. "I wonder if I'll ever get the chance to see it, now."

Sun cleared his throat, tapping his fingers lightly on his knee. Then, as if making up his mind, he said, "There is something interesting . . . As long you know about all this, I can ask your opinion."

He paused, and Marius said, "Sure, go on," encouragingly.

"Have you idea who would have stolen it?" Sun said, at last.

"Not any more than anyone else. I suppose it's a question of who'd stand to gain by it," Marius said, shrugging. "Maybe it was a political thing. That's what I heard. Or maybe somebody just stole it for profit. It must be worth a fortune, but it would be hard to dispose of, wouldn't it?"

"Very hard. As you know," Sun said, carefully, "I am not supporter of present Chinese government. But I am Chinese, all the same. I don't like see them lose respect."

"You mean you think they will lose face," Marius said, in Chinese.

"That is so," Sun replied, smiling. "I had forgotten how well you speak Mandarin. Please forgive me. Certainly, it is a matter of that unfashionable business of face. I know no one considers it nowadays, but for some of us it is still important. Besides, I am deeply involved with the Adjai. I think it would be a shame if the opening were spoiled or delayed. I am concerned about the British government as well—after all, I am a resident of this country. Well, for all these reasons, I would like to see the piece recovered."

He stopped again, took out a box of cigarettes—they were made for him by Sullivan Powell—and from another pocket, fishing for it with difficulty, a throwaway French lighter. "Be patient, Malius." Unlike Mei, he had trouble with his *rs*. "You know what we say, 'Open the door, see the mountain.' I am coming to the point." He lit his cigarette. "Yesterday afternoon, I had a visitor. He began by saying he had heard I was interested in buying works of art, especially ceramics. I said I was always interested if they were good."

"I don't believe it," Marius said, thinking of how Fitzhugh had approached him. "Did he tell you he had a teapot his uncle had left him?"

"Not at all." Sun appeared surprised.

"What did he look like?"

"He was very broad-shouldered, stocky, dark hair, a big head—"

"Okay. Never mind. Go on."

"And he was wearing a badly cut suit of hard material, not Savile Row, you understand. Even before he spoke, I knew he was a Russian."

"Oho!" Marius sat up.

"Then, from his accent, I was certain of it. He talked vaguely in circles—*beat the bushes,* you say in English—hinting that he had something very fine, a vase—"

"A vase!"

"You may believe I opened my ears when he said that. But, he said, he couldn't offer it around, he had to be careful, he was a foreigner and he had brought it into the country to sell, but he didn't want to call himself to anyone's attention. When I pressed him, he hinted that there was something slightly illegal about the whole thing. I asked him whether he knew anything about ceramics. How did he know that it was very fine, for instance? He replied that he knew a little, that he could assure me it was Sung Dynasty."

He leaned forward and deliberately crushed out his cigarette. "What do you think?" he said.

Marius pondered, chin in palm. "It might be the right one. But if the Russians have stolen it for political reasons, why would they come to you and try to sell it?"

"I considered that. Suppose they wanted to make it appear that the vase was stolen *not* for political reasons, but for profit? Then they might well try to pass it on to a dealer to throw suspicion away from themselves."

"Yes, that sounds reasonable. But how could they be sure you wouldn't recognize it?"

Sun lifted a shoulder. "How many people are experts? To them, one good vase would be much like another. Pictures of it have appeared in the papers, but no one has seen it except people connected with the museum, and as far as the public knows, I am not one of them. But I am only guessing. For all I know, this fellow may have been a professional thief who also just happened to be a Russian. And of course, it may not be the right vase."

Marius shook his head. "The only way to tell is to see

it. I don't suppose he had it with him, eh? That would be too much to ask. What did you say to him?"

"I told him that I also had to be careful, that I was a foreigner, too, and a respectable dealer. I didn't close the door—I hinted that I might be open to a deal—after all, I didn't want to frighten him away. I asked him to bring the vase to me here, but he said that wouldn't do, that I should visit him. He gave me an address—79 Starkey Gardens. I looked it up, it is in Chelsea. He told me to ask for Mr. Sergeyev."

Marius got up restlessly and went over to peer at the Huang P'ing-hung painting without really seeing it.

"Jesus!" he said, in English. "You could be on to something. It's worth following up. What about the cops? Shouldn't you get in touch with them?"

"I don't think so. You know police, Malius. They come with cars, bring search warrant, want to look for vase, and it's easy these people get rid. Bang! they break, with hammer, that's the end of it. Right?"

"I guess so." Marius nodded, his resolve already forming. "Okay. Now, listen, Chih-mo. Are you going to follow this up? Are you going to the address to see what he's got?"

Sun slowly moved his head from side to side. "Suppose they make trouble and I have to run? I am not built for it."

"So you're not going to do anything?"

Sun waved a hand. On the table near him stood a wide porcelain dish in which a miniature garden had been planted, a dwarf pine, moss, a rock, a tiny crane with its wings spread. "I am busy with *p'en ching,*" he replied. "That's what I am going to do. But if you want do something, good. That's why I told you."

Marius picked up his case. "Thanks a lot," he said.

"That's one way to get rid of a headache—transfer it to someone else. I'll let you know what happens."

"Are you going now?" Sun's face was not made for worry, but he succeeded in projecting a shadow of apprehension. "Be careful. I am glad a younger man is dealing with this problem, but remember this may be dangerous. I would like you to return and buy the painting."

"Put it aside for me. I'll see you," said Marius.

Sun watched him go. When the door had closed, he threw himself back in his chair and began to laugh. Everything had worked out exactly as he had hoped. He moved his chair closer to the table, picked up a little sharp pair of scissors, and began to cultivate his garden.

Chapter 7

Starkey Gardens, S.W.10, was a street which had seen the wheel come full circle. Its four-story houses, all with stone flights of steps leading up to a side-lighted front door, and mansard roofs with dormer windows, had been built for middle-class families in comfortable circumstances, but not quite rich enough for Belgravia. Then, between the wars, they had moved to the suburbs and their domains had been carved up into flats and flatlets and shabby bed-sitters occupied by shabbier lodgers, who were content to live in what had once been sculleries or nurseries, or who settled whole tribes in former drawing rooms and dining rooms. Now, the new expense-account middle class, its pockets full of pumped-up pound notes, was moving back in, restoring the cracked plaster, knocking out partitions to recover the spacious chambers, replanting the rank gardens.

Marius stood hesitantly before number 79, trying to decide how to make his approach. He was beginning to wonder if he should have ignored his first impulse and phoned Fitzhugh after all.

He had considered that, right after leaving Sun's gallery. He had imagined the secret agent's surprise: What? You're on to something so soon? Good work, Mr. Kagan, you'll get a medal for this. But would it actually go that way? The fellow would more likely be casual about it, touching the small moustache with the tip of his finger, sighing wearily, saying with a patronizing air, Yes, all right, we'll look into it. And suppose it came to nothing and Marius appeared a gullible idiot? Suppose it wasn't the right vase after all and a lot of trouble was stirred up for nothing? He remembered with annoyance how he had had to look up at the taller man, and with that his determination had strengthened to follow up the lead on his own and maybe even recover the vase by himself.

From the street in front of the house, however, things looked a little different. He might be walking into disaster. He had dealt with shady characters before, many times, but never in quite this way, in a case with international repercussions. Who knew what they might do? Send him to Siberia, never to be heard of again? I can't afford that, he grumbled to himself, and I have a date with Mei.

What it really came down to was that he simply couldn't, at this point, turn away, telephone Fitzhugh, pass the information on to him, and forget about it. It would be admitting cowardice and defeat. He took a firmer grip on his briefcase, noting that his palm was oily with sweat, and went up the steps to the door.

The man who answered his ring looked like Genghis Khan crammed anachronistically into a dark suit that didn't fit properly. He had a broad, harsh Mongolian face, with a fringe of moustache around his thick lips, but the collar of his jacket stood away from his neck and the sleeves came almost to his knuckles. He said nothing, just looked at Marius.

Marius said, "How do you do? My name is Marius Kagan. I'd like to see Mr. Sergeyev."

"You come in, please," said the man, in a light, pleasant voice that no more went with his face than his jacket did.

Marius entered a long hall lined with engravings of London in the eighteenth century. The other man opened a double door into a large front room with a polished floor reflecting a living room suite in Selfridge's best Finnish Modern style, complete with glass-topped coffee table, white goatskin rug, and Formica bar. The walls were hung with engravings of Paris in the eighteenth century. He indicated one of the chrome easy chairs.

"You wait, please," he said, and went off. Marius sank into the chair, the plastic cushion of which gave off a huff of indignation.

He had barely had time to find a comfortable angle in which to sit without all the loose change falling out of his trousers pocket, when another man came in who, to Marius's experienced eye, was suffering from a hangover. He was broad-shouldered and sturdy-looking, with a snub-nosed, wide-mouthed face which normally might have been both cheerful and engaging; however, the whites of his eyes were bloodshot, and he carried his head with dreadful care.

In fact, if anything, Alexei Sergeyev felt even worse than he looked. He felt as if he were made of very thin, fragile glass already fractured in several vital places. It was all because he was patriotic. He had gone to a dinner the night before which had lasted until three in the morning, and had been compelled to prove that a Russian could drink anyone else under the table. Oh, we Slavs, why are we so boastful? he thought, looking mistily at his visitor, whom he at first took to be a Red Indian. Ostap had said he was an American.

"Good afternoon," he said. "I am Sergeyev. I am

afraid I am rather busy. What did you wish to see me about?"

Marius, after a struggle, had succeeded in getting out of the chair. "I'm sorry to bother you. I am a friend of Mr. Sun, the Oriental art dealer. I'm a dealer in Chinese art myself, you see. And Mr. Sun told me you had been to see him, that you had a good Chinese vase for sale."

Sergeyev made his way to a straight chair and sat down slowly on the edge of it. "Excuse me, I have headache," he said, both because it was true and because he wanted a moment to think, once the words *Chinese vase* had penetrated his fog.

"Yes," he said, at last. "I have Chinese vase, but not for sale."

"I see," Marius said, uncertainly. "Well, no, actually I don't. I mean, you went to Mr. Sun and told him you wanted to sell the vase, didn't you? Now, he doesn't want to take a chance on handling something that might be hot, but I don't mind. So if that's what's worrying you, forget it."

"Is not worrying me," Sergeyev replied. He stood up, wincing as his head threatened to fall off, closed his eyes for a moment, and then continued, "I have vase safely, where you will not find it. It will," he said, dramatically, "never fall into hands of imperialist war-mongering clique." He thought that was rather good, and repeated, "War mongers. Yes. And since now you are here, you will not leave."

He felt in his pockets, clicked his tongue irritably, and added, "Excuse me." Going to the door, he called, "Ostap! *'Davai mnye pistolyet'.*"

"Wait a minute," Marius protested. "What the hell do you mean?"

Sergeyev flapped a hand at him, soothingly. A moment

later, the Mongolian type came in holding a large automatic, which he pointed at Marius.

Sergeyev said, "Now, Mr.—er, you will follow this man. Ostap, take him to top floor and lock him in."

Ostap motioned with the pistol. Marius picked up his briefcase.

"I don't know what you think you're doing," he said, trying to remain calm, "but you won't get away with it."

Ostap moved threateningly. Marius went past him and into the hall, wondering whether he dared make a grab for the gun and deciding that he didn't. As he left the room, Sergeyev uttered a long sigh. Then, pinching his temples with thumb and forefinger, he went to find an Alka Seltzer.

Marius, at Ostap's urging, climbed the stairs to a broad landing. His brain was in a turmoil; he could not shake off the feeling that what was happening was unreal, but there was nothing imaginary about the solid tread of the man behind him, or the heavy metal of the pistol, which Ostap held as if he had plenty of experience in using it.

"Go on," Ostap grunted. "Higher up."

The stair continued to another landing with several doors, one of which stood ajar to show a bathroom. Then another narrower and steeper stair led to the top of the house where, at either end of a smaller landing, there were two more doors.

Ostap pushed Marius to one side. Holding him still with the pistol against his chest, he opened one of the doors and jerked his head. As soon as Marius was inside, he closed the door. Marius heard the uncompromising click of the key in the lock.

He was in a good-sized bedroom which had once been two small rooms and still retained the dormer window of each. Under other circumstances, he would have thought it a charming, airy room, with its striped wallpaper, its white painted woodwork, its engravings of Rome in the eighteenth century, and its view of back gardens. It was simply furnished, with a cot, a bedside table, a small chest of drawers, and a wardrobe.

Marius sat on the bed and tried to think clearly. This fellow Sergeyev could not be an ordinary thief, unless one could conceive of a thief taking the lease on a house in this neighborhood and settling in fairly permanently. He, and the Mongolian—and there must be others as well in a house this size—could only be secret agents. This was their headquarters, as Fitzhugh used the office in Maddox Street. On the evidence, it appeared the Russian secret service had more money than the British. They were obviously the ones who had stolen the vase, to drive a wedge between China and the West, as Fitzhugh had indicated. The thief had been Chinese and his accomplices, the dustmen, Westerners. But that goon, Ostap, could pass for Chinese. And the others would have been Slavs.

There was only one mystifying point. Why had Sergeyev offered the vase to Sun Chih-mo, and then refused even to show it to Marius?

There was an answer to that, not wholly clear, but still possible. Sun, although Chinese, had left China to live in the West. It could be presumed that he was an enemy of the People's Republic, like so many other well-to-do Chinese refugees. Marius, on the other hand, as an American, might be considered more hostile to the Soviet Union than to China. Indeed—and he found that the thought unnerved him—Sergeyev might even take him for a CIA man, and in that case, he might well be on the side of Britain. Well, if it came to that, he *was* working for a secret agent, in a way. Maybe the Russian knew he had been approached by Fitzhugh.

He had been so deep in thought, he had forgotten

where he was. Now, he got up and surveyed the room. His first task was to get out. If he stayed where he was, there was no telling what they might do to him.

He opened one of the windows and thrust his head out, wondering if he could yell for help, or throw down a message. There was no one who would hear. The back gardens were empty. Beyond them were the roofs of a mews, but they were too far away and too far down. He looked from side to side. The buildings in this block were all semidetached, that is, they had been erected in pairs, each pair joined together and separated from other pairs by walks leading through fences to the gardens. So there was another house attached to this one, and if he could get up on the roof he could cross over to the next and perhaps get into it. From this window, however, it was impossible, for the roof was made of smooth slates and pitched far too steeply. Up at the top it was flat, but there was no way to climb to that part unless he squeezed through the dormer window, got up on top of it, and so somehow managed to scramble to the rooftop. But if he slipped—he glanced down and shuddered. It was too gymnastic a feat, especially since he had no intention of leaving his briefcase and all its contents behind.

He prowled the room, trying the door just to be sure it was locked. It was. He recalled all those films in which people hurled themselves against doors and burst them open. This one was a good, substantial, late-Victorian job against which you were likelier to break your shoulder. He inspected the bed, wondering if he could take it apart and batter down the door with its frame, but it was a well-constructed metal one and wouldn't come apart without tools. In any case, he would make so much noise that before he could get the door down, Ostap and his pistol would arrive to see what was happening.

He looked into the wardrobe. It was full of someone's

suits, exhaling a tepid, sweaty smell. The chest of drawers contained some cheapish cotton shirts and some lightweight but scratchy woolen underwear. Marius toyed with the notion of tying the bedsheets together with suits and shirts to make a rope, but the image of one of the shirtsleeves ripping loose as he was halfway down was too uncomfortable.

Sooner or later, someone would have to come and bring him something to eat, unless they intended to starve him to death, which he doubted. The bedside lamp was made of brass, fairly heavy, and without its frilly pink shade would make a good club. He could hide behind the door and bash whoever came in. He visualized the scene—Ostap would enter, quite unsuspecting, thud would go the lamp base on his skull, and down he would go. Marius nodded, sourly. He had been in many a fight, but he had never hit anybody in cold blood, just like that, and he knew quite well he wouldn't be able to. Besides, what was much more probable was that Ostap would come in, guess at once that he was behind the door, and just laugh.

He sighed, despondently. If this were a woman's room, instead of a man's, there would be bobby pins around and maybe he could pick the lock with one. Someone had once told him you could pick locks with a coat hanger, and he opened the wardrobe and stared glumly inside, wondering, as he did so, why so many English houses had no closets. And as he looked, he began to grin.

He glanced at his watch. It was a quarter to six. Stripping the bed, he took out his pocket knife, a neat gold-plated object a woman friend had once given him for Christmas, and began cutting and tearing the sheets into wide strips.

Sergeyev, between his hangover and an emergency call which had come in from one of his operatives, had forgotten all about his prisoner. It was not until after seven that he remembered, and, full of remorse, sent Shchedrin, who did the cooking, upstairs with a tray of food and a bottle of vodka. Shchedrin unlocked the door and pushed it open with an anticipatory smile, having prepared in his head the sentence, in English, "A little something to eat." He saw the open window, the bed pushed close to it, the rope made of pieces of cloth tied to one leg of the bed and leading out the window. Distracted as he was, he noticed with irritation that part of the rope was made of one of his new Marks & Spencer shirts, as yet unworn. Leaving the tray, he ran downstairs to report to Sergeyev.

Almost before he had left the room, Marius heaved himself out of the wardrobe. Even though he was short, it had been a tight fit. For a minute or two he could hardly get his legs to work, for he had been cramped up in there for an hour, holding the door part way open, waiting for the sound of someone coming up the stairs. He hobbled into the hall. He could hear loud voices down below and knew that Sergeyev would probably be coming up almost at once to see for himself. He darted across the landing to the other door and softly opened it. As he had expected, it led to a front bedroom. He had barely closed it behind him when he heard someone coming up the stairs, two at a time.

Voices speaking in Russian, someone's deep laugh, the rasping of furniture being moved, people talking and going downstairs again. He was safe for a bit.

This room had one large window instead of two, a fixed sheet of glass and a casement at either end. It had another important difference, too, not in the room but out of it. Along the edge of the roof, a little way below the window sill, and stretching right across the fronts of both houses, was a stone cornice. It was perhaps two feet high and stood several inches away from the roof to provide gutter space. Marius saw at once that by climbing out, he could make his way along this space to the house next door where there was a corresponding window.

He waited no longer. He had brought along half of one of the shirts, and he slung his briefcase over one shoulder by it. He eased through one of the casements and let himself down cautiously until his feet were resting on the gutter. The cornice braced him and prevented his seeing the street below, which was a help. Leaning inward toward the roof and with his hands against the slates, he shuffled along with no trouble beyond one unpleasant moment when he had to climb over a stone ridge that separated the two houses. Both the casements were open in the neighboring window, and without a pause he climbed through the nearest.

There was a woman inside, frozen in the act of taking something from a bureau drawer, her mouth and eyes wide open in alarm.

"I beg your pardon—" Marius began, in his most charming voice.

With a wild screech, she fled from the room, slamming the door behind her. There was a sharp click. Marius was locked in again.

Chapter 8

Commander (C13) Percival Wilde tried for the fifth time to produce a light from his new cigarette lighter and then, in a passion, hurled it across the room. At once, he regretted the act; it did not accord with the calm, icy personality he preferred to show the world. Fortunately, no one else was present and without loss of face he was able to retrieve it, with a mental note to have a harsh word with his tobacconist first chance he got. When that chance would come there was no telling. C13 dealt with Special Crimes, and this one was not only undoubtedly special, it was one of the worst flaming headaches he had ever encountered.

He sat down again, found some matches in the top drawer of his desk, lit his cigarette, and looked at his notes once more. Nil. Everything nil. Whoever had stolen that bloody Chinese chamber pot had covered himself well.

At first, the thief himself, the man who had marched so calmly in and taken the thing, had seemed a likely lead: gray-haired and with glasses. This had blown when a pair of spectacles with plain glass lenses had been found in the museum basement, dropped or thrown away by the thief. It had then occurred to Wilde that the gray hair might have been a wig. As for other identification, well, one bloody Chink looked much like another. He had passed that problem on to his leg man, so far without result.

Then, the dustmen and their phony lorry. He had had men checking all the possibilities they could think of for rental, sale, or theft, but the trouble again was that there were no distinguishing marks. It had been a perfectly ordinary high-topped, one-and-a-half-ton van, the sort any number of small concerns or even market gardeners might have for their deliveries, of a perfectly ordinary dust color. It hadn't even been exactly the kind that usually came, but the guard in the basement hadn't thought anything of that; why should he? Wilde spent a moment or two in wistful contemplation of what he'd like to do to that guard. But after all, it wasn't actually the man's fault. The lorry had had, on its doors, the name of the contractor and there was no reason the guard should have been suspicious of a rubbish collector. The contractors, a firm in Camden Town, had been able to prove the whereabouts of all their vehicles on that day, and their regular collection at the museum, in any case, would have been on the following day. Forensic had been unable to come up with anything, not even a helpful tire mark or a fragment of paint. The spectacle frames had come from Woolworth's, and someone had fitted them with plain glass, but there wasn't even a clear fingerprint on them. A thorough investigation had been made of everyone connected with the museum, for someone on the inside must have known the name and collection times of the rubbish contractor, but so far nothing solid had turned up.

There was one minute piece of evidence, but as yet it led nowhere. The guard had exchanged a few casual words with one of the spurious dustmen. The man had

had an Irish accent. *IRA?* Wilde had written on his pad, and had circled it three or four times. One of those Palestinian guerrilla groups had had some Japanese helping them. Why not a Chinese working with the IRA? Somehow, the notion was so farfetched that it made his heart sink. What was more probable was that petty Irish crooks had been hired by the thief to act the part of dustmen, and were now safely back in Eire, there being no way to check the passage of people between Britain and the Irish Republic. Not for the first time, as he thought of that, Wilde felt a griping at his bowels, like indigestion; how could you control bombers who sauntered back and forth as they liked? But never mind that now. He had enough to think about.

His informants, usually reliable grasses, had so far found nothing. He had contacted several very good people, old friends in the East End who had connections with certain underworld characters, but the most diligent inquiry had drawn a blank. As for the liaison with the Chinatown gangs, that had produced even less. Drugs, yes, but the stealing of high-class art goods was not in their line and they were indignant at being suspected. A faint—a very faint—rumor had reached Wilde of a secret organization somewhere outside the known list of villains (he still liked to use the old-fashioned word for big-time crooks, although his younger assistants grinned at it), but so sealed was the Chinese community against outsiders that the whole thing was too vague to go on.

What else was there? Nil, zero. The Assistant Commissioner was beginning to make threatening noises, feeling pressure from the Commissioner, who in turn was hearing a certain amount of rumbling from the Home Secretary himself; the case might well have international repercussions, although thank heaven so far they had been able to get the papers to cooperate in keeping silent. "Surely, Commander, the government's position must be plain to you . . . embarrassment . . . alarm . . . cannot understand why you have not as yet been forthcoming with . . ." It was all perfectly plain. His was the head that would be spiked above the gate of New Scotland Yard to serve as a warning to all foot draggers. And as if that wasn't enough, he now had this flaming shit of a CIA man to deal with.

He glanced again through the fellow's file. Then he picked up the phone, pressed a button and said, "Bring Mr. Kagan in, will you?" By the time the door opened, he was his usual cold, reserved self, not a trace left of the cigarette-lighter-flinger of former times.

Marius, by now, had also recovered his poise and had his Agreeable Dealer Ready to Please face on. It had been a struggle, between confusion at trying to explain to the police—they had taken only a few minutes to answer the frantic telephone call of Mrs. Pargeter—what he was doing in her bedroom without going into too many revealing details, and also wanting to get to a phone to allay Mei's worries, for by the time he had arrived at the police station it was nearly eight. Then, once he had given his name, there had been various low-voiced consultations and some telephoning, and then he had been shipped off in the rear seat of a large dark-red Jaguar (aha! he had had time to think, I forgot that at least one English car is named aggressively) to Lambeth. There, while waiting in a chilly pale green anteroom, he had been able to persuade one of the policemen to phone Mei and tell her he was all right. At nine, he was thinking longingly of the tray of food that that Russian had brought up and which he had had no time to sample, and then he was shown into an office where a bald man with a heavy, brooding face sat behind a desk. The room was layered with smoke and smelled like an ashtray.

"Sit down, please," the man said, and added to the policeman who had brought Marius in, "You can go, Hughes."

Marius took the straight chair on the other side of the desk, and crossed his legs, looking alert but calm, as if in the sale room.

"Marius Kagan," the man said, shuffling some papers. "You're an art dealer from New York. Specialty, Chinese works of art. You make frequent trips to London, presumably on business. Don't look so surprised; we keep files on all regular business visitors, especially those in the art world. A necessary precaution."

"I see," said Marius. "Would you mind telling me who you are?"

"Commander Wilde. As for your other professional affiliations, I won't go into those."

"I don't know what you mean," Marius said, in surprise. "What other affiliations?"

"I don't want to know about them. That's between you and Fitzhugh. But I won't have you crashing around, upsetting civilians, climbing in through windows—you chaps think the law's made for everyone else, but it damn well isn't."

"But listen," Marius said. "Wait a second. You mentioned Fitzhugh. Are you involved in—" He didn't want to spill anything, mindful of Fitzhugh's warning, but at last said, "—a case concerning a certain vase?"

"You might say so," Wilde answered drily. "I'm in charge of it."

"Well, then, you're just the man I want to talk to. Look, the reason I was climbing in that window was that

I was escaping from the house next door, where some Russian agents were holding me. I couldn't explain things properly to the cops who picked me up because I didn't want to have to go into the story of the vase. I was told to keep it secret. But I know where the Sung vase is. It's in that house. The Russians have it."

There was a long silence, and Marius, who had expected his information to be greeted with a certain amount of animation if not joy, began to feel like a man who has told a joke with the wrong punch line.

At last Wilde crossed his arms and sat back with a faint sigh. "Do you know what time it is?" he asked.

"Eh?" Marius automatically looked at his watch. "Nine-fifteen. Why?"

"Because," Wilde said, sharply, "I haven't had anything to eat since eleven this morning. Now, look here, Mr. Kagan. I'm not having this. Your world of grand international intrigue may be jolly fun for you, but I want to remind you that I'm dealing with a crime, and in England, at any rate, crime is the responsibility of the police."

"I'm not quarreling with that," Marius cried. "That's just why I'm telling you what I know. Don't you want to get the vase back?"

"Very well. How do you know it's in the house of the alleged Russian spies? Did you see it?"

"Well," Marius said, reluctantly, "no. But the man I spoke to made no bones about it. He told me he had it. He said, and I quote, 'It will never fall into the hands of you capitalist war mongers,' or something like that. What's more, he had his buddy hold a gun on me and they locked me into an upstairs bedroom. Is that specific enough for you?"

"Yes," Wilde said. "Suppose he had told you he had

the vase, and had then shown you the door? Would you have swallowed it?"

"I—" Marius paused and thought. "Maybe I'd have been suspicious and thought he was bluffing."

"So should I. Particularly with that nonsense about capitalist war mongers. I imagine he threw it in because it sounds something like the dialogue in an American film. The best way to persuade you that he really had it was to hold you prisoner, for a time at least. I don't imagine—granting that your man was really a Russian spy—I suspect they are fairly intelligent—I don't imagine for one minute he was astonished at your escape, however you managed it. I should have thought—and mind you, I'm only a stupid policeman—that if the Russians actually had the vase, they'd be careful *not* to say so. Or don't you agree?"

Marius grunted.

"I believe your escape would have been contrived one way or another, eventually, so that you could get out with the information that they had the vase. Doesn't that seem a reasonable possibility?"

He leaned back in his seat, looking faintly pleased with himself, and Marius yearned to push him over backward.

"Right, Mr. Kagan. I think we understand each other. From now on, please stay out of my way."

"I was just trying to be helpful," Marius said, sullenly.

"I appreciate that. I don't mean to be harsh, just realistic." He had relaxed enough to sound a trifle friendly. "However, I suspect that by now the vase is serving as a doorstop in some shebeen in Dub—" He cut himself off abruptly, in some annoyance.

Marius said, "Dublin? Why Dublin?"

"Just a figure of speech," Wilde said, beginning to get up.

"You've got some kind of lead, haven't you?" said Marius, in a chatty tone. "Is the IRA mixed up in this, too?"

"Certainly not. And don't say 'too.' If you've managed to convince me of anything, it's that the Russians had nothing to do with the theft. They are simply taking advantage of it. I think we can forget the political side of it. Any professional thief would naturally capitalize on our thinking it was political. In any case, I don't want to see you again. Is that clear?"

He went to open the door. "Good night, Mr. Kagan," he said.

Marius said, "Good night," and went to retrieve his briefcase from the policeman in the anteroom. He was already wondering how he was going to find a cab at this hour, in Lambeth, and so he did not notice Wilde jerk his head at a swarthy man in plain clothes who sat unobtrusively in a corner, nor did he see the swarthy man nod in reply.

He managed to get a cab in spite of his misgivings, and on the way tried to sort out his thoughts. It was useless; all he could think of was food. Mei met him with a worried kiss, and even as she was asking him if he was all right, he said, "I'll tell you everything later. What's to eat?"

"Some things too late to make. I cook you something quick."

"Okay, fine, go ahead. Anything will do. I'll make myself a drink."

She got to work, neatly and efficiently as always, while he poured himself some whisky. Sipping it gratefully, he stood at the kitchen door watching her.

"You were in trouble with police," she said, stir-frying thin strips of beef and vegetables.

"That's right." He began to wonder how much he could tell her. He didn't want to drag her into something that might be dangerous, but on the other hand he was beginning to have some ideas about the robbery, and Mei, intimate with him as she was, a Chinese, someone he could trust, might be the one person who could help him.

"I hope is not something bad."

"It's something I shouldn't talk about."

She darted a strange glance at him, quick and penetrating. "Something secret?"

"Yes. But I'm going to tell you about it, Mei. Only you have to promise me you won't breathe a word about it to anyone. It could be—well, I don't want you to get hurt."

She had heated the rice and she filled two bowls and put them on the little kitchen table. "We eat in here," she said. "It's nice and cozy. You want some wine? Sit down."

She poured some Liebfraumilch—she had no taste in wine at all—and with her chopsticks put some meat and vegetables on his rice. She always served him this way, making sure his bowl was full of tidbits, whether they were at home or in a restaurant. Marius said it was the Jewish mother in her.

"You tell me what happened," she said, beginning to eat.

"You know about the Sung vase the Chinese government has sent over for the opening of the Adjai Museum?"

"I saw pictures of."

"Well, it's been stolen. Whoever was behind it, the actual thief seems to have been a Chinese, working with some Westerners. They disguised themselves as dustmen, came to pick up the museum's rubbish, and the Chinese walked in and took the vase."

"Wasn't it locked up in case?"

"Yes, but earlier that day the keys were taken from the man who had them. So the first thing is that somebody knew the name of the contracting company which was picking up the museum's garbage." With his chopsticks, he ticked off the points on his fingers. "Two, they knew which days the pickups were supposed to be made. Then, as soon as the keys had been stolen, the rest of the operation was put into motion and the truck was sent off to the museum. All clear, so far?"

She nodded. "And you know who stole—and why?"

"No. I wish I did. But you can see it might have been done for political reasons, to make both Britain and China look bad. If the story gets out—well, you figure it, a man walks right in past all the security and walks out with the vase and nobody can find him. The Chinese government will be in a rage and naturally won't lift a finger to help, because it's Britain's ball game. If the museum opens without the vase that's going to be a big blow to good relations between the two countries. I thought it was possible the Russians did it. And this seemed to be borne out for me. You know Sun Chih-mo —of course you do."

"I know."

"He told me he'd been approached by a Russian who offered him a Sung vase. The man had given him an address, so I went there and sure enough, the place was crawling with Russians. The fellow I talked to said yes, he had the vase and wasn't going to give it up. Then he had me locked in a room. I got out by a trick—never mind what, now—and got into the house next door.

They called the cops and I was arrested for housebreaking."

He laughed at the memory, for now that he had had something to eat, he could see the funny side of it.

"So you sure the Russians have it? What you going to do?"

"I'm not sure the Russians have it. The policeman in charge of the case pointed out to me—something I hadn't thought of—that if the Russians had it they'd be careful not to say so. They just wanted me to *think* they had it. It figures, doesn't it? They're against this entente between China and the West. So if they don't have the vase, they'd want to protect whoever did steal it, and the best way to do that would be to make me think *they* had it."

He wagged his head. "Complicated, but makes sense. And it started me thinking. What about Sun?"

"What about?"

"What if he's mixed up in this?"

"Why you think that?"

Marius laid down his chopsticks, and leaned towards her. "Just consider it, Mei. Somebody in the museum knew about the garbage men. Sun's there a lot these days, and he could easily find out something like that. What if the whole story about being approached by the Russians was so much crap? What if he put me on to them to cover up the real thief?"

Her face was impassive. She watched him and said nothing.

"He's no friend of the Reds," Marius went on. "He's a rich man, he left China ahead of the revolution. Why, he could be a Formosan agent! That would explain it. If I could only find out a little more about him. That's what I was hoping you could tell me."

"I can tell you something about him," Mei said, in her

own language. "I am certain he is not working for Formosa. I know some people who are very close to him, and they have told me where he gets some of his money. From the People's Republic."

Marius goggled at that. "For the Reds? My God, I can't believe it."

"It is true."

"But he left China before 1949."

"So did others, who have now been converted. But he has relatives there still. You know how important the family is to us."

"I always thought his family had either gone to Singapore or come to London with him. I remember him telling me that, once."

"He was lying. And it is easy for men to change, especially when there is money at stake. I don't say he is a Red agent. But his position makes a good front behind which he can help them."

Marius rubbed his forehead with the heel of his hand. "If you're sure—well, that lets him out. It means the Russians went to see him, hoping he'd pass on the word they had the vase, so as to divert attention away from whoever the real thief was."

He picked up the chopsticks, but instead of eating rapped out a little tune with them on the edge of his bowl. "If not the Russians," he mused, "then who? Do you know anybody who's tied up with the Formosans? They must be the ones, unless it was done as a private job after all. That's what Commander Wilde thinks."

"I know people who are in favor of the Taiwan government," Mei said. "But none can be secret agents, they are all business people. I don't think there are any Formosan spies here in London. They are—" she fluttered a hand, vaguely, "over there, in the East. There is another possibility, my dear, but perhaps you will think it's too farfetched."

"I've reached the point where I'll listen to anything. Go on."

"Maybe," Mei said, carefully, "the Russians were playing a double game with you. Could they not say loudly they have the vase—you will think they haven't got it—but really—"

"—they have it after all. Oy! Mei, darling, I don't even want to think about that." He lifted his bowl and skillfully scooped the last of the rice into his mouth with his chopsticks. With his mouth full, he said, "What I want you to do for me, honey, is just check around and see if you can find out who might be tied up with Taiwan. The Chinese might not talk to me, but they will to you. And there's another thing. Among all the Chinese in the catering trade, there may be some who hire Irish workmen."

"Irish?" She stared in astonishment. "Who would do that?"

"That's what makes it so interesting. Who, indeed? Can you ask around for me?" He snapped his fingers. "I just had a thought. I know somebody else who can help me. Somebody who owes me a favor."

"Who?"

"You wouldn't know him. Will you try to find out what you can for me?"

She sat back, picking her teeth with a toothpick, covering it with the other hand, one of her habits Marius found diverting.

She said, "I wish you would not go on with this."
"Why not?"

She snapped the toothpick, her head down. Then she bent close to him, her dark almond eyes grave.

"You are getting into something—there is so much danger."

"What?"

She had used the word *hsien,* but he had been staring at her and had missed the tone so that she seemed to be saying something about thread.

"Danger, Marius," she replied, in English. "I say there lots of danger. You get hurt maybe. And what for? What you care about China or Britain?"

She clasped his hand, convulsively.

For a moment, he thought to himself that she was right, and then his pride, or pure stubbornness, rose up. If he quit at this point, especially after being ticked off so contemptuously by that policeman, Commander Wilde, he would never be able to forgive himself.

"I have to," he said, curtly. "No, I'm sorry, I shouldn't have sounded so sharp. I can't go into it, Mei, it's too complicated, but I just have to keep at this thing. Don't worry about me. Nothing's going to happen."

He patted her hands. "This whole damn thing has spoiled our evening, but we'll try again tomorrow. Okay? Meanwhile, will you try to find out what you can for me, about, you know, the Formosans, or about anyone who might have hired some Irishmen?"

"All right, I try. You not staying tonight?"

"I've been climbing in and out of windows, and been hauled all over the place, and given a hard time by Russians and English cops—and it's midnight. I have to be up early, and I've got someone coming to the hotel first thing tomorrow. What about tomorrow night, are you free?"

"I have business meeting until late, but we go to a restaurant after. You want to go one Mr. Young's places, the Gallery maybe?"

"That'll be fine. You make a booking, and I'll meet you there at seven."

He got up, stretching, and kissed her tenderly, each eye, her cheek, her mouth.

"Don't worry," he said. "I can cope. On the outside I may be just an art dealer, but inside I'm a quaking mass of jelly. No, honestly, I'm tougher than I look. Appearances are deceptive—you know what that means?"

"I know," she said, in a small voice.

All the way back to the hotel he thought about her, and about the two of them. What's to become of us? he asked himself. How the hell are we going to work this out?

Now that he had found her again, he knew how hard it would be to let her go, even harder than it had been before. Yet they were no closer to a solution. Nothing had changed. She would not give up her business and move to New York; he was more determined than ever —now that Britain had a whole battery of new, increased taxes—not to make it his base. Even Tom Bridger was talking about emigrating, and Henry Shipton, an Englishman whose specialty was lacquer and porcelain, had settled in Japan. But he couldn't part with Mei. Perhaps they could live six months in England and six months in America? Perhaps they could find some mutually agreeable ground—Hong Kong? Kyoto? Honolulu? He turned it over again and again in his head, but all that happened was that he grew even wearier than he had been, until his thoughts wound down and he found himself repeating nonsense syllables. He recalled the story Mei had told him about the Heavenly Weaver, and thought about the Bird Bridge and about magpies. Funny, he thought, how cultures differ: magpies in some parts of England are thought to be bad luck, but in China they are the bird of happiness, *hsi chüeh*. The word rattled round and round in his head as he paid off the cab and went up to bed.

Chapter 9

Nothing but the urgency of the situation would have got Guy Neuville out of bed that morning. Even so, it was a fearful effort. He had had some very peculiar dope, given him by Ahmad the night before, and had actually felt his substance unraveling, spinning out into a long rope of ectoplasm full of giggles, and he had had far too much wine and far too much rolling about with Ahmad and that bird whose name he had forgotten, although he could still see the ring of dirt around her neck and smell her rank smell. Thank heaven, he had decided to go home by himself, forcing himself to remember that he had to be at the Comus by nine-thirty and in reasonably good condition.

That, old boy, he told himself, shutting off the alarm clock, proves the power of the will. There's still something left in me after all. He surveyed the squalid bedroom—clothes heaped on chairs, scratched furniture, cabbage roses on wallpaper blotched with dampness—shivered, and dragged himself out of bed. If all went well, he could put an end to this filthy way of life and start afresh.

He drank some water and took a shower. He couldn't face breakfast and made some instant coffee, very strong. He rooted among his clothes, wondering what would most impress the American, and at last got out a very good Irish tweed jacket, almost unrumpled, dark gray flannel bags, and one of the shirts made for him some years ago by Petty, a lovely creamy Egyptian cotton which he wore with the collar open and a silk scarf tied under it. This was an outfit he hadn't worn in heaven knew how long and as he brushed his hair before the glass he was taken aback by his own appearance, strangely youthful, even dashing. After a moment, he went searching through the toilet chest and eventually found a pair of nail scissors with which he laboriously trimmed his beard, making it shorter and more pointed. He now looked, he thought, something like a Middle European poet who had fled to Sussex to escape Communist verse forms, and he threw the scissors petulantly into a corner, but then began to laugh. The American wouldn't know the difference. If anything, there should be leather patches on the elbows of the jacket, but it was too late for that.

The American. Once again, Neuville congratulated himself on his perspicacity in listening at the door of the office when Patrick had been on the telephone. He had a lovely old-fashioned gadget which he had found useful before this for such purposes, a nineteenth-century auscultator, not six inches long, which some kindly country doctor had once used to listen to his patient's chests. If he were ever searched, no one would ever guess what the thin, trumpet-shaped piece of wood was for. And so he had been able to hear the details about Marius Kagan, an interesting name, with the faintly comic flavor American names all seemed to have. But there was nothing comic about his connection with the CIA.

As he set out—it was no more than a twenty-minute walk from the shabby neighborhood of Praed Street to the elegance of Grosvenor Square—he tried to consider how best to handle matters. Fitzhugh had given him £50, a down payment he had called it against the 200 Neuville had asked for, and for which he was to find out exactly what the Chinese wanted of him. That, at any rate, had been easy enough: Ch'in had made it clear that they were interested in whatever details he could pass on of the Russian organization. After the meeting with Kagan in the restaurant, however, he had been able to stall; he had also not yet reported to Fitzhugh. There would be time enough to decide which side to play on after he had sounded out the American.

But you couldn't just walk in and say, "I want the CIA to employ me in the States." They'd back off, of course, suspecting penetration, a double purpose. No, he'd have to approach it obliquely, get Kagan's interest, hook him. He still had nearly £30 left. If it turned out that some sort of cover was needed for this meeting, or subsequent ones, he could sacrifice it in a good cause. And there was another sacrifice that could be made. Poor old Patrick, it was a shame to play such a dirty trick on him, but since this Kagan was already in contact with him, and knew him to be a British agent, he would provide the best offering.

Neuville unbuttoned his jacket, for the morning was growing a trifle warm for tweed, and strode on in good heart.

Marius, in fact, was not very impressed by the new image. In the sunlight which streamed through the tall corner windows of the sitting room of his suite, Neuville looked less prepossessing than he had in the restaurant. The faint greenish thread running through the jacket, the yellowish cream of the shirt, brought out the biliousness of his complexion and the discoloration of his eye whites.

Furthermore, his beard looked oddly lopsided as if an unfelt wind were blowing at it from one side. However, there was no denying the excellence of the materials of his clothing, and if he appeared dissipated that might only mean money, with whisky at about $8 the bottle.

"Glad to see you," Marius said, shaking hands. "I'm afraid I can't give you too much time, though. I have a number of business calls to make this morning."

"What a pleasant old place this is!" Neuville exclaimed. "One of the last of the good old English hotels. Yes, I quite understand, Mr. Kagan. And of course, I can only be a minor sort of customer if at all. I'm afraid I know very little."

"I understand. You're not obliged to buy anything, you know. But you were talking about tomb figurines the other night. Now, I haven't any of those here in England with me, but I can show you a few amusing little jades."

He had some finger pieces, a Buddha's-hand citron, a bear, two bats, a mythical *ch'i lin,* nothing extraordinary but well carved and of good quality. He laid them out on the desk for Neuville.

"They're charming. Did they have some purpose?" Neuville said.

"Pick them up, handle them. They're delicious to the touch. That's their purpose."

"Marvelous! How much is this fat little bear?"

"Two hundred pounds."

Neuville laughed. "Good Lord! And he's such a tiny thing. Appearances are deceiving, eh?"

As he said this, he gave Marius a pointed, meaningful look. Marius was remembering that he had said something very similar to Mei the night before, and grinned.

"Yes, I know what you mean."

"Do you?" He rubbed the cool, oily jade with a

thumb, still eyeing Marius. "Now you take me, for instance. I know I look as if I hadn't a serious thought in my head, but do you know what my profession is? I'm an electronics engineer."

"Is that so?"

"I'm freelancing these days, as a consultant, but I've worked for a great many important firms and I have a good many contacts in the field. Much of it is defense work—armaments, computer miniaturization, servomechanisms, that sort of thing. I've often thought my specialty might be useful in America."

"I suppose it would," Marius said, with an interior yawn.

"Yes, you see, I do get around. I meet all sorts of people and a lot of sensitive information goes from hand to hand. I often get the chance to intercept it. I'm sure if I could find the *right company*—" He lingered over the word, knowing its inside meaning. "Such a company in the States might be able to make use of me."

"Well, I hope you find it," Marius said, politely. "Would you like to see some bronzes?"

"I like this bear," Neuville said, recognizing that he was being parried. The man must understand him by now but was being cautious. "Oh, damn. I've come out without my checkbook. Suppose I give you a deposit? Shall we say twenty-five pounds? Then we can meet again when you have a bit more time, say at my place, and I'll pay you the rest and you can show me any other little things. Naturally, I won't take the jade with me. After all, you don't know me from Adam. Although," he added, "we may have some acquaintances in common. One of them might vouch for me."

"Oh, that won't be necessary."

"No, no, I'm sure there must be someone. Have you

run into a man named Patrick Fitzhugh? He gets around a lot."

Marius blinked. "Fitzhugh? Do you know him?"

"Oh, yes. We've *worked* very closely together. Of course, on second thoughts, it might be better if you didn't mention me to him. I know some very—well, how shall I put it?—*embarrassing* things about Pat." He laughed, beginning to enjoy himself, for he could see from Kagan's expression that he was getting through.

"What kind of embarrassing things?" Marius asked, in bewilderment.

"That would be telling, wouldn't it? And I ought to point out that Pat isn't the only one. As I told you, I have a good many interesting contacts. Does the name Calthrop mean anything to you? But I'm sure I needn't say any more. I'll leave you to think it over, and we can discuss it in more privacy when you come to see me. What about this Winnie-the-Pooh, then?"

He took out his wallet and counted out five £5 notes, not without a pang, reminding himself, however, that he'd be holding a £200 jade hostage. "I'll take the bear along, shall I? Or," he added, with a laugh that still held traces of an earlier charm, "perhaps you'd rather not trust me."

"No, of course I trust you," Marius said. "Take it. But—"

"I know, you'll want my address." Neuville found his pocket diary, tore a page out, and wrote. "There's my telephone number, as well. Shall we say tomorrow night? Make it on the late side, say after eleven, and then we won't be disturbed. I'm sure we can work out some future profitable deals. And you do understand that it would be much, much better if I went to America?"

"Oh, sure I understand," said Marius, who had by now

realized that he had to do with a real, old-fashioned, demented English eccentric.

"Splendid! Good-bye, then, until tomorrow night."

Marius remained gazing at the door for a minute or two after it had closed. Then he picked up the money and the piece of paper, although he had still not altogether decided whether for a $400 sale it was worth dealing with a nut.

The mention of Fitzhugh, however, had reminded him that he wanted to talk to the man. Putting aside, for the moment, the small-world coincidence of Neuville knowing him, he fished through the masses of cards, old envelopes, and scraps of paper on which he had written notes, until he found the bit of pasteboard which said, *Electrodyne Research Co., Ltd.* He dialed the number backward, as he had been told.

A voice said, "Yes?"

"Can I talk to Mr. Fitzhugh?"

"Who's this?"

"Marius Kagan."

"Oh, right, guv'nor. Hold on a tick."

After a moment, Fitzhugh came on the line. "Yes, Mr. Kagan, what is it?"

"I thought maybe I ought to talk to you," Marius said. "I've found out a few things you might be interested in, about that—you know—you asked me to keep my eyes open. Do you want me to tell you what I've learned?"

"Where are you?"

"I'm in my room at the Comus."

"I see. No, don't say any more over the phone. Could you possibly come here this morning?"

"Not this morning. I have some things to do. What about this afternoon?"

"That will do. What time?"

Marius looked at his schedule. "How about five?"

"I'll expect you then."

He hung up, and Marius, taking his briefcase, went out into the morning to make some money.

He was able to put the Sung vase and its complications out of his head for most of the day. About four, he got out of a taxi on Shaftesbury Avenue and strode to Gerrard Street and the bustling district of Chinatown.

He hadn't been here in over a year, and it seemed to him that the neighborhood was beginning to lose some of its character, with the encroachment of Western shops and restaurants. But there was still enough left to give it its special flavor. In front of the Hong Kong Cultural Services a group of people waited among suitcases and parcels, staring into the windows of the noodle shop where a cook was ladling hot pork into bowls. Shoppers streamed in and out of the Loon Moon Supermarket with its ranked bottles of Fritillary & Loquat Cough Mixture, Royal Jelly, and Essence of Chicken and Cordyceps. Behind the glass of restaurant after restaurant hung the shining carcasses of ducks and sides of smoked pork, and even at this hour there were plenty of diners, for the filling of the stomach played a central part in Chinese life. In one bookshop there was an immense photo of Bruce Lee in color; in another, stirring titles like *The Foundations of Leninism,* and *Forty Red Hearts Are with Chairman Mao Forever* stood at attention. The movie posters trumpeted an adventure about the Boxer Rebellion, while a splendid piece of calligraphy in bold *hsing shu* script advertised what in Chinese are called "yellow" films, and in English, "blue."

Marius threaded his way among the crowds. The young men wore their hair long, trying to look as much like Bruce Lee as possible, with flowered shirts open to the navel and gold chains around their necks. The older men, in spite of the warm weather, wore dark coats and ties, and shirts with stiff white collars. Girls in summery prints or blue jeans chattered loudly, and here and there a woman in the old-style Cantonese jacket and trousers walked behind her husband as if the world had not changed. Among them drifted the tourists with their cameras, the most foreign of foreigners here.

Marius went round to Lisle Street, where the Chinese section halted abruptly, halfway along the street, at a sex shop which advertised "Erotic Sounds for Adults." The boundary, just before it, was marked by a narrow shop filled with junk jewelry, kites, incense burners, badly faked T'ang horses, framed pieces of garish needlework, and copies of a popular booklet called *The Water Mirror Too Good to Be True Fortune Teller.* There was no shop sign, but on the inside of the window a square of cardboard read, "Good Nature Wang Practically Gives Things Away."

Inside, a young man with a sullen face was reading a grimy copy of *Playboy,* which he put down reluctantly when Marius entered, keeping his place with a finger.

"I want to see Mr. Wang, please," Marius said.

"Not here."

"I'm sure he isn't," said Marius, with an edge to his voice. He took out one of his business cards, and handed it over. "Will you show him this, please? I'll wait."

The young man looked at Marius's stony face and went away through the beaded curtain at the back of the shop. He returned, looked considerably chastened, and said, "Please go down, sir," standing aside and holding the curtain for Marius to pass through.

A flight of steps led to the basement, where there was a door marked *Private* standing a little ajar. Marius pushed it open and entered a room full of the noise of the sea breaking on a shingle beach. It came from half a dozen mah-jong tables. The players, men and women, were all Southerners, cheerful, noise-loving, and they snapped their tiles down with decisive clicks or scrambled them round and round to shuffle them, so that it was as if hundreds of pebbles were rattling together. When Marius came in few of them glanced at him, so concentrated was their attention, but one man, who had been sitting a little apart from one of the games, got up and came towards him, holding out his hand.

Wang Lai had the typical Cantonese face, with knobby cheekbones, a short, wide-nostriled nose, a lurking air of merriment. His skin was pitted by smallpox; he was gray-haired and wore thick steel-rimmed spectacles. He shook hands energetically, taking off his glasses as politeness required, exclaiming, "Ah, Mistah Ka-gong, I not see you long time."

Marius made no attempt to speak Chinese, for Wang understood Mandarin no better than Marius did Cantonese. "It's good to see you, Mr. Wang. Can we sit somewhere private? I want to talk to you."

"Oh, yes, we talk." He said something to the people at the table where he had been sitting, and led Marius to another door. Behind it was his office, a quiet, small room in which a faint odor of sandalwood clung, furnished with a rolltop desk, some straight-backed wooden chairs, an old iron safe, and a delicate piece of calligraphy in grass-style writing which quoted from Mencius, "Benevolence is man's mind and righteousness is man's path." Wang bowed, motioning to a chair, and when Marius was seated, sat down himself and with a smile took a bottle of whisky and two small cups from a drawer.

"I not forget you," he said, in his heavily accented English. "Now you like drink?"

They had first met years before, when Marius, strolling

idly, had seen in the shop window among the junk a very good Ming ivory seal and had bought it without bargaining for about a quarter of what it would have fetched in the sale room. On subsequent visits to London Marius had dropped in to visit him, had bought things which from time to time fell into the other's hands, and had even played mah-jong in the parlor downstairs from which Wang made a fair living. Then, one day, Wang had asked for some advice. He had a very beautiful album of what looked like high quality paintings, but he didn't know enough about art to be able to judge whether they were originals, and there was no other dealer—not even, or especially, the Chinese—whom he trusted. Would Marius help him? The album was by a famous seventeenth-century painter, and Marius got a couple of other opinions, sold it for a very large sum to an American collector, and took only the smallest of commissions.

"Why you not come see me?" Wang said, handing him a cup.

"Lots of business," said Marius. "I just haven't had a minute when I've been in London, lately. How have you been? Well?"

"I pretty good. Make lots money but pay lots tax. You buy good things?"

"A few. That calligraphy is new, isn't it?"

"I get from somebody owes me money."

Marius peered at the signature and seals. "Pu Yi—he was the last Ch'ing emperor. What's this date?"

"Suppose be 1920."

"Poor kid, he was Mister Nobody, an emperor on half-pay. He wrote a pretty good hand, though, didn't he? I suppose," Marius went on, sitting down again and toying with his cup, "you meet a lot of people who still long for the old days, the time of the imperial rule, even though it never did anybody any good except the rich."

"You right, no good for anybody but Mandarin. But now, Reds no good for nobody at all." He laughed, a high-pitched giggle, bobbing his head. "What you want? World all gone to hell, nobody make living. I don't care which side, I on one side only, Wang Lai."

"Yes. You can do me a big favor, Mr. Wang."

"I do. You tell me what."

"Well . . ." Marius had been trying to decide how to envelop his request in a plausible story but could think of nothing. He plunged on, "You know everybody around here. What I want to find out is whether there's some company, a Chinese company, which would have a good-sized van or truck—I mean, a lorry—and which might hire Irishmen to drive it or work on it."

Wang stared at him out of eyes that had suddenly gone opaque.

"You understand what I mean by Irishmen?" Marius asked.

"I understand," Wang said, at last.

"They wouldn't necessarily use Irishmen all the time. They'd have hired them last week, and probably only for a day. But maybe this is too hard for you to find out," Marius ended, for Wang was certainly looking very blank.

However, he seemed to pull himself together. "Why you want to know?"

"It's for a friend. He—ah—he has an Irish friend he's trying to find, and he thinks he may have worked for a Chinese firm."

"All right," Wang said. "I find. But must be careful. Must be very careful, because Chinese businessmen don't like too much question. You know?"

"A secret," Marius said. "Right. Of course. Thanks very much."

All the usual merriment seemed to have gone out of the little man. He rubbed his hands nervously, so far forgetting politeness as to stand up and make a jerky motion to the door.

He said, "You come tonight, I tell you something. But must come late, very late, when everything shut up and nobody see you. All right?"

"Okay," Marius said, getting up as well since his host had done so. It was obvious that Wang was worried; clearly, the notion of asking prying questions was repugnant to him. Marius felt a twinge of remorse, but it was too late for that now. He said, "What time? About midnight?"

"Later, later. Maybe two, three o'clock, after nobody eat in restaurant, everything shut, nobody on street. You come?"

"Three o'clock," Marius said. "It's a hell of a time, but if that's the way you want it, I'll be there."

"I don't want people know I talk you," said Wang.

"I understand. I'll come here to the shop—"

"No, not here. You go Gerrard Street, on corner Nassau Lane. I meet you."

Marius shrugged. It seemed to him that Wang was carrying caution pretty far, but after all it was he who had asked the favor and he had to go along with the other's wishes.

"I'll see you," he said, as Wang threw open the door with something like relief. "And I do appreciate this."

"*Ch'i kan*—I am not worthy," mumbled Wang, with a bow.

Marius went upstairs into the shop, realizing that he was going to be late for his appointment with Fitzhugh.

It was, however, not very far to Maddox Street across Soho. He stood for an instant, planning the best route, and as he did so his eyes came into focus, as it were, and he saw through the dirty glass of the door a man standing across the street on the corner of a lane running down to Leicester Square. He was studying a London guidebook, a typical tourist with a camera slung over his shoulder, but Marius had seen that face before, that Cary Grant chin, the clean-cut features, even the sunglasses. It was certainly odd how the fellow kept turning up. It crossed Marius's mind that it might be too much of a coincidence. Was it possible someone else had put a tail on him? It was faintly ludicrous to think of two of them following him around. Still chuckling, he left the shop, ignored the man with the sunglasses, and struck out through the home-going crowds.

He was let into the office by Fitzhugh, looking more worn and haggard than ever and smelling slightly of gin. Perhaps it was owing to the gin that he seemed more amicable.

"Ah, Mr. Kagan, come you in," he said. "I'd begun to wonder what had happened to you."

"Sorry I'm late. I had somebody important to see. I may be on the track of something."

"I see. Good." Fitzhugh led him into the inner room and shut the door, leaning back against it for a moment, closing his eyes. "Things have been a trifle chaotic. Please sit down. Can I offer you a cup of tea?"

"No, thanks."

Fitzhugh sat down opposite Marius at the table and brought out his cheroots. "You don't smoke, I seem to remember. We may as well get down to it. What was it you wanted to tell me?"

Marius couldn't resist beginning, "Well, since you've

had a guy following me you know where I've been. But maybe you don't know what happened inside some of the places I've been in."

Fitzhugh did not return the smile. "Go on," was all he said.

Marius went on. He told about his talk with Sun Chih-mo, the meeting with Sergeyev, and about his escape from the house. Only at the mention of Sergeyev's hangover did Fitzhugh's lips twitch.

"So when the cops came," Marius concluded, "they took me to Lambeth, and eventually in to see a fellow named Wilde, Commander Wilde. I suppose you know who he is—he told me he was in charge of this case."

"So he is—from the police end."

"Then you know he doesn't think much of your idea that this was a political crime. He was sure the Russians didn't have the vase. He was convinced they only pretended to hold me prisoner—even though it was a pretty good pretense—to hammer home the belief that they did have it. He thinks the thief took advantage of the fact that everyone would expect it to be a political theft. But I suppose you know all that."

Fitzhugh, fiddling with his moustache, longed for a drink. But there was only a drop left in the bottle, and if he brought it out he'd have to give some to this stunted clown. It had been some consolation to hear that Sergeyev was human, anyway, and could have hangovers like anyone else. It was also clear that Sergeyev had taken advantage of a situation which had been offered to him. Fitzhugh himself had had only one quick meeting with the Russian at the very outset of this affair and had had no other opportunity to brief him about Marius. He now began to consider how to make the most of what had happened.

He said, at last, "I'm familiar with Commander Wilde's views. I don't share them. Like most policemen, he tends to be very narrow. And there are a good many things he doesn't know and can't know. In the first place, that chap C. M. Sun—I can tell you something about him. He gets his money from the Americans."

Marius's jaw didn't actually drop open, but he felt as if it had. "You're joking," he said.

"It's quite true," Fitzhugh said, smoothly. "Like a good many Chinese who are opposed to the Reds but aren't actually connected with the Formosans, he has undercover ties with the CIA. Very useful to them, you see. He can collect information and pass it on, since he has contacts both here and in the East."

Marius opened his mouth to say he had been told that Sun was an agent for the People's Republic of China. He closed it again. For if he said that, he would have to say who had told him, and he didn't want to get Mei mixed up with a British secret service agent. Besides, her information was probably no more than rumor; this man must know what he was talking about.

Fitzhugh went on, "I'm sure the Russians don't know this, however. I have reason to believe they think Sun is working for the Formosans." This, at any rate, was perfectly true; it was what he thought himself, and had passed on to Sergeyev long before. "That would explain why they approached him, you see. They would have felt they could get the vase into safe hands, and out of their own."

"But why would Sun have told me about it?" Marius asked, in some confusion.

"There, of course, I'm not certain. But it may be that Mr. Sun took you for more than you appeared to be."

"More than—"

"Just put your mind to it, Mr. Kagan. You told me that when you met with him, you told him you knew all about the theft of the vase. You're an American. He may have jumped to the conclusion that you were with the CIA."

"Me?"

"Why not? You'd make a good CIA man. You travel freely from one country to another, and your business provides a perfect cover."

Marius gazed at him in stupefaction. "But that's ridiculous! Isn't it? Maybe it isn't."

"That's right," Fitzhugh said, complacently.

"But then—then you think the Russians really have it?"

"Let's say I'm reasonably certain."

"And when that man Sergeyev told me he had it—"

"Well, I imagine you startled him. He didn't know whether you were working with Mr. Sun, or with the CIA. Naturally, he'd have to lock you up until he could make sure."

Marius looked about him helplessly, kneading his forehead. Then he gave a humorless laugh. "How the hell did I get tangled up in this? I never should have listened to you. So now I'm an American agent, am I? Of all the fucking—"

"Calm down, Mr. Kagan. There's no need to be upset."

"No need? Jesus! I'll bet that cop, Wilde, thought I was one, too."

"Oh, no, I shouldn't think so. He simply thought you were meddling in things."

"He was right, wasn't he? I'm leaving. The hell with your plots. I'm taking the first plane out to Paris."

"I can understand your consternation," Fitzhugh said, and added, in a murmur, "A man in your position would naturally be frightened—"

That stopped Marius as nothing else would have. He sat back, folding his arms.

"It's got nothing to do with being frightened," he said, coldly. "I'm a businessman. I just don't want to find my business cut out from under me."

"I assure you it won't be," Fitzhugh said. And then, since this was no time for half measures, he added, "Would you like a drink?"

"I wouldn't mind. What have you got?"

"Only gin, I'm afraid." Fitzhugh got up and went to the bureau. "And nothing but water."

"That'll do."

Fitzhugh poured him a small one and took a somewhat larger one for himself, masking their sizes with the water, his back to Marius. They both drank, in silence.

Then Fitzhugh said, "You've really been awfully helpful, Mr. Kagan. What you've told me has taken me one step closer to the truth. If you can just be patient and go on a little longer. . . . Once we've found the vase, I can see to it that everything is cleared up for you. There'll be no trouble."

"What do you want me to do, then?"

"Just go on as you have done. You see, it's just as I had hoped, just as I told you at our first meeting, you are finding out certain things for me. Because of your special position you're attracting information, so to speak, which I can't possibly get hold of."

Feeling a bit more relaxed, Marius was able to remember his talks with Mei and Mr. Wang. "As a matter of fact," he said, "I may be on to something else for you."

"Really?" Fitzhugh tried to sound as gratified as possible.

"Yes. Wilde let something slip, something he obviously didn't want me to know. He covered it up, but it started me thinking."

"What was it?"

Marius grinned. He now had an opportunity to pay Fitzhugh back for that crack about being frightened.

"I'd rather not talk about it yet. It may not come to anything at all."

"Perhaps you ought to let me be the judge of that," Fitzhugh said, a little too brusquely.

"Perhaps," said Marius. "But why don't you just play along with me? I'm following it up through some—through a friend of mine. It may be just horseshit, but if it comes to anything I'll have a real piece of news for you."

Fitzhugh's lips tightened. "I think you're being very unwise."

"I guess so," Marius said, airily. "I'll try not to let it scare me."

He got to his feet. "So long. I'll keep in touch."

"You do that," said Fitzhugh, forcing a pleasant note into his voice. After all, the little bastard was so touchy, one had to be careful with him; he just might take his information to Wilde, and that would wreck everything.

Marius went down the stairs and out into the street with something of the buoyancy of one who has just finished a session with the dentist. Apart from his dislike of Fitzhugh, there was a sense that the air in that room was charged with tension. It arose partly from the feeling that Fitzhugh was a little too carefully playing the part of a seedy ex-military man, as if even the toothbrush moustache were false, and something of his exertion in maintaining the role communicated itself. But also, it came from the uneasy recognition that he, Marius, was becoming enmeshed in something considerably bigger and more threatening than he had ever anticipated. It wasn't only Fitzhugh who was acting a part. There was falseness and double-dealing all around him. That Russian, Sergeyev—it was impossible to guess what he had really meant, or what his real motive had been for imprisoning Marius. And an even bigger shock had been the revelation that his old friend, Sun Chih-mo—whether Mei was right, or Fitzhugh—was not what he seemed. And still worse, it now appeared that Marius himself, involuntarily, unsuspectingly, might have been an actor in the same play, might be taken for what he wasn't.

He shook himself. There was no point in trying to get it all straight, he was in too deep. He could only plough on and see what happened. And not alone, he reminded himself, wryly; he was being tailed by one, possibly two, men. Maybe more—maybe that cop, Commander Wilde, had sent someone to watch him. And what about the Russians? "My God," he told himself, "I may be dragging half a dozen snoopers behind me all over London!"

He walked westward towards his hotel, whistling a song that had been popular when he was a boy: "Me and My Shadow."

Chapter 10

No shadow of worry clouded Mei at dinner; it was as if they had never discussed the theft of the vase. Restaurants always excited her. She chattered vivaciously, half rising to reach across the table with her chopsticks, arguing with the waiter about the preparation of dishes, turning constantly in her chair to see who was coming in or to exchange greetings with friends, the dimples under her eyes punctuating her smiles.

"You are marvelous," Marius said. "No, I don't want any more rice. Listen, how about moving to Hong Kong?"

"I don't want live there. I like it very much, and you know I still have uncle there, with his family. But what I do about Richard, leave him here?"

"Why not, for God's sake? He's a big boy. What is he now, twenty-one?"

"I like London," she said, obstinately. "Why you don't move here? You have no son, no family to worry. Maybe you don't like English food?"

"I don't like English taxes." He gave her more tea and went on, moodily, "We're not getting anywhere. I'm trying to find some middle ground, Mei. Some place where we can both be happy and carry on our business."

"I don't know where," she said, with a sigh. "Your trouble, you have no home. You live in New York and do your work there, but nothing else holds you there. If you had home—"

"I do have a home. You've never seen it. I have a whole house on a charming, pleasant street without muggers—well, anyway, not very many. There's even a room Richard could have, in the basement, with his own private entrance. Look—why don't you at least come over with me when I go back, and just see what it's like? I'll pay your fare."

"Maybe. I think about. When are you going?"

Marius grimaced. "That's a good question. Probably on the seventh or eighth, but I'll have to go to Paris first. You could come with me, couldn't you? We've never been in Paris together."

"I like Paris," she said, and dropping her voice, added, "You can't go until that thing found?"

"No."

"Have you find out anything else?"

"Not yet. That reminds me, about tonight—I have to see somebody at a hell of an hour, three in the morning."

She pretended to frown. "Oh, you have some other woman, eh?"

"Yes, a dazzling eight-foot blond. You silly wench. You remember, I told you I knew someone who owes me a favor? I'm going to see him. He's promised to try to get some information for me."

"Who is he?"

"Nobody you know, a junk dealer. What about you? Have you learned anything?"

"Nothing." She drank her tea, and looked into the cup, cocking her head like an inquisitive bird. "If you have to get up at three, why we don't go to your hotel?"

"Instead of your place? I don't know, a hotel is—" He wrinkled his nose.

She grinned. "You don't want the hall porter look at

you. I know. You think everybody watch us coming in and wink at each other, and they say, 'No, you can't take woman upstairs,' and then we have embarrassment."

"That's not it at all," Marius said, uncomfortably. "It's just that—it's just—oh, hell. I don't want people to think—"

"What you care what people think? It doesn't make any much difference to *me* what they think. They all strangers anyway, so it's none of their business. You have guilty feelings because you think is a sin to make love to somebody you not married to, but Chinese people have no religion, only Tao, and so we are realistic. We think by rationalism. You know, Mencius says man is born pure, and if he is put to the black he becomes black, if put to the red, becomes red. That means people only become bad if they live in a bad way. So we have no guilt inside because we have no idea of Original Sin, that idea that man is born guilty."

Marius grinned in spite of himself. "You're talking about Christians," he said, "but I'm not a Christian. We Jews conduct our business with God on a direct line, and we figure we can always talk Him around."

"I know. But you live in Christian world, and you manage because you don't make it trouble."

"Well, okay, but what's the rationalist point of view about going into a hotel and having the hall porter think you're bringing in a hooker?"

She threw her head back, laughing. "What is hooker —a whore? If you think I'm that, it makes me one. Is that what you think?"

"You know better than that," Marius said, stung.

"So then what you care what's in his head? In a hotel like the Comus, you rich Americans pay for him keep his thought to himself. If he says anything, you don't give him nice fat tip. Only in cheap hotels they worry. Don't be middle class, Marius."

He reddened. "I was only thinking about you, Mei, not me."

"I thought would be easier for you, go from hotel, then come back and you get some sleep and be there for business in the morning. But if you don't want—"

"No, I really don't mind, if you don't."

They had no plans for after dinner, and when Marius had paid the bill they strolled out through the Soho streets, hand in hand, taking delight in the provision shops where a hundred cheeses were marshaled rank on rank, the overcrowded liquor stores offering TO-DAY ONLY bin-ends of undrinkable Provençal wines, the bookshops aflutter with pornography, the shop which rented gold-framed copies of famous paintings for television plays, the shop which sold tools for left-handed people, and the ubiquitous strip joints where spotty girls drearily undressed themselves six times a day.

They came, eventually, to Oxford Street, all but deserted now, and stopped at the lights of the tube station beside a late newspaper stand on which the placards announced, NEW BOMB OUTRAGE IN MAYFAIR 2 DEAD. Mei wanted to go home, first, to get her nightgown and toilet articles, and after some debate they caught a bus as far as Marble Arch. A man sprang out of the shadows and jumped on the bus with them, a swarthy fellow in a dark suit; when they got off, he got off with them and walked around the corner. They crossed the Edgware Road and struck off towards Mei's building, and when they were in the lobby Marius, who had been glancing back surreptitiously over his shoulder said, "He was following us."

"Who?"

"Didn't you see that guy who was on the bus with us? He pretended to go the other way but I caught sight of him behind us. He's another one."

"What you mean another one?"

"I've already got two people tailing me. This is a new one. For all I know, the other two are out there too, somewhere."

Mei said nothing while they were in the lift, but in the apartment, when Marius went to the balcony and looked down at the street, she said, "Maybe you better have drink. You very nervous."

"Is that so?" he said, coming back into the room. "I'll have a drink, but I'm not imagining things. There's somebody across the street, up against a building, having a quiet smoke. I don't know which one, we're up too high."

He drank a little neat whisky, while Mei peeped around the corner of the french window.

"I see him," she said, "but are you sure he's watching for you?"

"I'm sure. One of them's a short, hook-nosed fellow, and the other one wears sunglasses. And now one who looks like a Mafia type. It's a wonder they don't bump into each other, crowding around in the street. It's a Goddamn bore." He put his glass down with an irritable thump. "I know one thing. We're not going to have them chasing us to the hotel. Is there a back way out of this building?"

"I don't know."

"Well, we'll find out. Come on, get your stuff together."

She packed a few things into a more capacious handbag. As she was about to turn out the lights, Marius said, "No, leave one lamp on."

They descended in the lift to the basement. An echoing passageway smelling of cement ran the width of the building. One arm ended at the janitor's flat. The other, passing a couple of closed doors, led around an angle to a steel door marked *Exit*. Stepping through, they found themselves in a paved area lighted by a small iron-bracketed lamp at each end, and bordered by a row of garages belonging to the tenants. Driveways led out at either end to the street in front of the building, and to a smaller, narrower one behind the garages.

Marius, fixing in his mind the position of Mei's flat and remembering where he had seen the watcher, caught her by the hand and drew her towards the further driveway. For a breath they were under one of the lamps, then they had slipped around the corner of the block of garages and into the shadowed driveway. They emerged in the back street and stood there, listening.

"I think we've lost him," Marius whispered, his lips close to Mei's ear.

He glanced up and down the street they were in, but there was no sign of any other watcher, only a woman in a white coat walking a wheezing, overfed dachshund. Marius slipped Mei's hand under his arm and they crossed to the darker side, and so, by one turning and another, went northward until they found a cruising taxi. Once inside it, they collapsed against each other in a fit of giggling, like a pair of teenagers.

This lighthearted mood lasted them all the way to the hotel. The hall porter did not even glance at them, although Marius mentally dared him to raise an eyebrow. They went into the bar and sat sedately over their drinks, a small manzanilla for Mei and a large malt whisky for Marius. A fat man in a glaring houndstooth hacking jacket was talking to a smaller man, holding him by one lapel with a meaty fist, and as he talked he rocked from his toes to his heels, pulling the other back and forth with him; the smaller man's face was turning green with seasickness. This started Marius laughing again until he began to hiccup, and he sat blushing, holding his breath with his hands above his head, while Mei buried her face in her handkerchief. They left their drinks unfinished and fled upstairs, and in the dark warmth of bed, still laughing, embraced.

Marius had set the alarm for two-thirty. He shut it off quickly, but Mei awoke and said good-bye sleepily before turning over again. He dressed in the sitting room so as not to disturb her, and then, snapping off the lamp, parted the drapes a little way and looked down into the street. He could see no one. He remembered having seen Fitzhugh's man sheltering in a telephone box, but the three boxes on the traffic island in front of the hotel were empty. He went downstairs.

The lobby was dark except for a floor lamp and the shaded light at the hall porter's desk. The porter himself was dozing in his little glass-walled room and did not stir. Marius let himself out and stood under the canopy, surveying the street once more. If the men who were following him were there, they were well hidden. He concluded that either they were still watching Mei's apartment house, or had gone off to get some sleep.

Except for a few clubs, or student hangouts, London is an early city and Marius, at that hour, had the streets pretty much to himself. He had allowed fifteen minutes to dress and another quarter of an hour to walk to Gerrard Street, and he did it easily, having no traffic to wait for, no crowds to thread through.

There was a street lamp at the corner where he had been told to come, but no sign of Wang Lai. Marius stood under the light and looked at his watch. It was a couple of minutes past three. Surely he couldn't be considered late?

He looked about him. It was eerie, to be alone where earlier that day there had been so much activity. The shop signs were off, the shops gloomy caverns behind their windows, the doors padlocked. A single pallid bulb burned in a restaurant, silhouetting the corpses of glazed ducks strung like a curtain across the window. The cold, white, electric glare of the street lamp made a pool about Marius, emphasizing his loneliness and the silence. At intervals along the street other lamps stood sentry. Across from where he waited, Nassau Lane ran into gloom; behind him was the darkness of a large, empty lot. There was no sound except for the occasional muted rush of a car a little distance away on Shaftesbury Avenue.

Then suddenly, shatteringly, a motorcycle exploded into life. It came from somewhere behind him in the lot, racketing louder and louder, and Marius, startled out of his wits, jerked himself back against the lamp post, turning to face the noise. It was this involuntary movement which saved him. The motorcycle roared past him missing him by an inch or so. He had an impression of wheels, of chrome, of a helmeted head, and then it was gone, down the street.

"You son of a bitch!" Marius stepped away from the lamp post, out into the street. He shook his fist, enraged at such carelessness, only dully taking in that under a far lamp the rider was heaving his machine around, only slowly comprehending that it had not been an accident, and then the thing came hurtling at him once more. The blank plastic windscreen of the rider's helmet caught a flash of light; he was faceless, rigid, as if he were no more than part of the machine.

Even then, Marius could not altogether grasp what was

happening. He hesitated, and only at the last moment leaped aside. The motorcycle tore past, the handlebar grazing his arm. It skidded around the corner into darkness.

Marius ran, in terror. He ran to the lane opposite, stumbled, fell against a high wooden wall. It gave under his weight, with a creak. He realized first that it was a pair of doors, second that they were unfastened. He pushed harder, a crack opened, he slid between the leaves and shoved the doors shut behind him. There was a bolt and he saw, now, that it had been closed but had not engaged in its locking slot. He pushed it shut and fastened it just as, in the street outside, the noise of the motorcycle broke out again.

He heard it growl to a stop. He could imagine the rider searching for him, the faceless mask turning from side to side. He looked about him for some escape.

On this corner, there had once been a small building. Its brick walls still held, crumbling, to its neighbors, and the wooden gates had been built across the open end to make a parking place now nearly filled by a delivery truck. Beyond the nose of the truck in the back wall, Marius could see a door. He edged along the side of the truck. He was wearing rubber-soled shoes and they made no sound, but he put each foot down carefully, biting his lips, trying to still the hammering of his heart. He could hear boots clacking in the street. Then someone tried the wooden gates, and he could hear them rattle.

He shrank back against the cab of the truck. He thought if he could get into the truck he might find a jack handle or a wrench, something that would do for a weapon. His hand was on the handle of the cab door, when he heard the footsteps outside again, and then the splutter of the engine being kicked on. He guessed that his attacker must have thought he had run into Shaftesbury Avenue. The motorcycle roared, moved off, dwindled.

Marius stayed where he was for a while, straining his ears. It might be a trick to lure him out into the open. At last, he went softly to the door in the far wall. It was locked. He returned to the cab of the truck, weighing the thought of a weapon, and as he stood there irresolutely, he saw something that made him catch his breath, that put all other thoughts out of his head.

The light from the street lamp spilled over the top of the double wooden gate, and raked the cab of the truck. It illuminated the legend, *Gow Yok Trading Co., Ltd.* on the side of the door. But because of its slanting rays, it showed, too, that something else had once been painted underneath those letters, then covered hastily, and the *Gow Yok* part painted in again, for the second legend overlapped the first unevenly. Between, and showing faintly, he could make out BRA . . . DON . . . RUBBI . . . EMOVA . . . CONTR . . . AMDEN TOW . . .

He stared, filling in some of the spaces: *Bra*—somebody—*Rubbish Removal*—and then *Contractors? Contracting?*—and *Camden Town* perhaps? He pinched his eyes shut, thinking back to what Fitzhugh had originally told him. He had said, "The museum contracted with a small firm in Camden Town to collect their rubbish."

Marius went around to the other side of the cab. It was in shadow, but he passed his fingers over the door. Sensitive to the textures of ceramics, he felt, or fancied he could feel, the slight raised surfaces of the letters below the legend *Gow Yok Trading Co., Ltd.* which he could just make out. In daylight, you would never see the repainting except, perhaps, as a slight difference in color.

There could be no doubt of it. This was the truck which had been used in the robbery.

There could be no doubt of something else. Wang Lai

had something to do with it in one way or another. He had clearly shown his perturbation at Marius's request, and he had insisted on this meeting at so late an hour so that someone could make the attempt on Marius's life. Marius's questions had cut uncomfortably close; it must have seemed he knew more than he actually did, and so Wang—or someone to whom he had reported—had decided to get rid of him.

So much, he said to himself, clenching his teeth, for gratitude. Whom can you trust?

He went to the gates and pressed his ear against the wood. Still no sound from outside. He couldn't stay here all night; he would have to take a chance on leaving. He was already beginning to feel slightly ashamed of the fright which had gripped him, and he saw himself, in fancy, knocking the rider off his motorcycle, making some sort of stand, instead of running blindly. On the other hand, he reminded himself, if he hadn't run he would never have found the truck.

He pulled open one of the doors and stepped out. He was alone. He started away, and reminded himself that if they found the gate open tomorrow, they'd know he had taken refuge inside and know, also, that he'd seen the truck. He fiddled with the bolt and was able to arrange it so that the end of it was touching its receptacle; then, when he pulled the leaves of the gate shut with his fingernails, the bolt slid into place. It was at least no worse than it had been at first, and to anyone coming from inside it would look as if the doors were bolted.

He looked at the buildings on either side. Above an entrance on Nassau Lane was the sign, *Gow Yok Trading Co., Ltd.* in English and Chinese, and in the murky windows below an assortment of packaged herbs, candies, foodstuffs, and cheap porcelain. It would be interesting to know who the owners of the business were. Could Wang be one of them?

He began walking, still apprehensive, expecting that at any instant the motorcycle would come racing out of some hidden alley, but nothing happened. It wasn't until he was nearly back at the hotel that the thought struck him that they might try again another time. It made his stomach lurch with sudden, sickening fear.

He opened the door of his suite softly, so as not to wake Mei, but as he went in thought she must be up for a lamp was lighted. As he shut the door behind him, the smile he had prepared froze. There was a man in the room staring at him in equal petrifaction.

Marius recognized him even without his sunglasses—the clean-cut young executive face, the Cary Grant chin, and even in this situation, his jacket unrumpled, his shirt crisply white.

"What the hell—?" Marius began.

"Sorry," said the other, in that odd, mumbling voice which sounded like loose teeth. "Must be the wrong room. Got mixed up—a little too much to drink—"

"Mixed up?" Marius said, his anger rising. He looked at the bedroom door. It stood wide. There was no sign of Mei.

Before he could say anything else, the other man, with a false smile, started to thrust his way past him to the door.

"Just a second," Marius said, grabbing at him.

The man swung at him and punched him, glancingly, on the arm, the same arm the motorcycle had grazed. Twice in one night was too much. Marius lost his temper.

With a snarl, he sailed into the other. He hit him in the chest and, as the man tried to hold him off, again, on the point of that beautifully cleft chin. The man staggered backward, fell over an armchair, and sprawled, whooping and gasping, clutching at his throat.

Marius suddenly realized that he was strangling, probably on his dentures. He dragged the fellow up on his knees and beat him between the shoulder blades. A curved piece of plastic flipped out of his mouth on to the carpet.

"Whoo!" the man said. "Thanks."

Marius turned the piece of plastic over with his toe. "What's this thing?"

"I—well—" The smooth executive cheeks burned. "It's a voice changer." He was no longer mumbling.

"I see," said Marius. He put a foot against the other's shoulder and shoved. Unbalanced, the man fell over. "Now, unless you want me to, one, beat the shit out of you, or two, call the cops, you'd better start explaining. What did you do with the woman who was here?"

Seated on the floor, the other stared up at him. Marius, fighting mad, had a hot eye and a dangerous look, short as he was.

"There wasn't anyone else here," the man said.

"You're lying."

"I'm not. Sorry. If she was here, she went out. I got here about ten, twelve minutes ago. I thought you were —well, you know, at her place, because that's where you were the night before last, and I saw you go there earlier tonight."

"All right, now you tell me who the hell you are, and why you've been following me."

"You don't know?"

"No, I don't know. Stop crapping around."

"You're not in any other division?"

"I don't know what you're talking about."

The man's eyes shifted from side to side. Marius went to the desk and picked up the straight chair.

THE CHINA EXPERT

"Don't even think about trying anything," he said. "This chair feels nice and solid and ought to make a good crunch on your head."

"All right, all right. Central Intelligence," said the other. "And you're not?"

Marius slowly put the chair down, and after a moment, sat on it.

"What do you mean, I'm not?" he said.

"Well, we know you've been in contact with the British side. And then we had the tip that you were with us, only nobody knew who you were. We thought you'd been sent in without notification, you see, and then we weren't sure so I was told to keep an eye on you."

"You knew I'd seen Fitzhugh?" Marius said. "You thought I was with the CIA?"

"Sure. You were obviously working on that Chinese vase caper, and we'd been told to keep our hands off it, that it wasn't any of our business. So we couldn't figure what you were doing."

"So you were searching in here for some clues to who I was?"

The other nodded. "Can I get up now?" he said.

"Yes. Get up and get out, will you?" Marius grunted.

The man got up, and as he did so took from some hidden holster a stubby, nasty-looking pistol which he pointed at Marius.

"Another one!" Marius exclaimed, in disgust.

"That's better," the man said. "Now talk. Who are you?"

"You could have asked me that in the first place. I'm a dealer in Chinese art. I was asked by that British agent to give him a hand, to identify the vase when they find it, and to see if I could dig up any information he could use. I've been hassled around so much I just don't give a damn about any of this any more. Okay?

Now, why don't you go away and let me get some sleep?"

"Just hold still," the other said. He came behind Marius, held the muzzle of the pistol against his back, and deftly searched his pockets. He looked through his wallet, his credit cards, the accumulation of notes written on scraps of paper. Then he moved away.

"You seem to be clean," he said, doubtfully. "I believe you, I guess. For the time being, anyway. But as an American citizen, you shouldn't be working for British intelligence."

"I'm not working for British intelligence. And I'm not working for you, either."

"Okay, friend. No hard feelings." The man tucked his pistol away and scooped up the voice changer from the floor. "Good night," he said, cheerily.

"Yeah," said Marius. "You can tell your boss he can take you off my ass, because I'm quitting tomorrow."

He watched the door close on the fellow. He looked at the floor, where the contents of his pockets lay strewn about his feet. There was a slight noise from the bedroom, and he lifted his head. Mei stood in the doorway, in her pajamas.

Marius was beyond surprise. "Where have you been?" he said.

"I was hiding in bathroom," said Mei. She came to him, putting her arms around him gently. "Are you all right?" She began picking up his things, which he crammed back into his pockets.

"I'm okay. I don't understand anything, that's all. You were hiding—?"

"I heard that man come in and I thought was you. When he put the light on, I saw him. I jumped up and hid behind the shower curtain, in bathroom. I heard him moving in bedroom—the drawers opening and closing—then after a while I heard you talking to him when you came back. I saw you fighting—"

Marius rubbed his face hard, with both hands. "Oh, yes, this has been a really delightful evening," he said. "A guy tries to kill me with a motorcycle, another guy frisks me at the point of a gun—"

"What you mean?" She caught him by the shoulders. "Who tried to kill you?"

He held her away. "Take it easy," he said. "I'll tell you about it, but before I say another word I'm going to have a drink."

He had a bottle of Glen Grant on a side table, with glasses and a pitcher of water, and he helped himself to a stiff one, noting angrily that his hands were shaking. Mei hovered, watching, her face drawn and pale. At last Marius put down the glass.

"The man I thought was going to help me is a dealer named Wang Lai," he said, wearily. "Do you know the name?"

"It's a common name," Mei said. "Maybe I know."

"He runs a mah-jong parlor and keeps a junky art shop. He told me to meet him on a street corner tonight. He never showed up, but someone on a motorcycle tried to run me down. He came damn near doing it, too."

"*Ai!*" she exclaimed. She clasped her hands together, pressing them to her mouth. "Now I see. You get too close to something."

"That's what I figured. I told Wang I was looking for someone who owned a truck and who might have hired some Irishmen. Well, I got even closer than they know, whoever they are."

He told her about finding the truck. "Have you ever heard of the Gow Yok Trading Company?" he finished.

"I know name. They on Nassau Lane."

"You don't know who owns it, do you?"

"I don't know. Some businessmen, I suppose. I don't do business with it."

"It's obvious that they're more than just happy-go-lucky businessmen," said Marius, sourly. "A whole lot of things are clearer, now. For one thing, everybody seems to have the idea that I'm working for the CIA, including the CIA themselves. That's why Sun sent me to the Russians, and it's why the Russians tried to make me believe they had the vase, according to Fitzhugh. And now I know for sure they haven't got it, whatever Fitzhugh says. I had forgotten something. According to the Chinese guard who saw the thief, he looked like a Cantonese. If that's so, he couldn't have been a Russian, nor would the Russians have hired the Irishmen to work the garbage truck.

"It's obvious that whoever owns the Gow Yok Trading Company hired the thief and his accomplices. Chinese, not Russians. So it's obvious, too, that it's the Formosans who were behind the robbery, and who tried to kill me."

"I don't believe not," Mei said, haltingly. In times of stress, her English sometimes disintegrated. She drew a long breath, and then she did something Marius had never seen her do before. She went to the side table, poured out half an inch of whisky, and drank it in two swallows.

Then, in Chinese, she said, "It was not the Formosans who were behind the robbery."

Marius's mind was still on the astounding spectacle of seeing her drink whisky, and he couldn't adjust to the change of language. "What did you say?" he muttered.

"It was not people from Taiwan who stole the vase."

"What makes you think that?"

"I don't think it, I know it." She came close to him, took his hand, and held it against her breast. "Mah Lissu." She used the Chinese version of his name as a caress. "I want to tell you something, but I don't want you to be hurt, or angry. I work for the Formosan government."

The blood rushed to his head, and his ears began buzzing. He pulled his hand away from her, and said, thickly, "I don't understand what you're saying. Say it in English."

"Please, don't be angry, Marius. I know is shock to you. No, I can't say—my English no good when I feel it this . . . I am an agent of the Formosan government. It would not have made any difference between us until tonight, until you were nearly killed, and now I see that I must help you."

He shook his head as if plagued by flies, waving a hand in front of his face. Then he said, harshly, "Let me get this straight. You're a spy, is that right?"

"That is so."

"No, damn it, talk English! I don't care how tough it is, I don't want to take any chances of misunderstanding you. How long have you been working for Taiwan?"

"Long time, four, five years. My husband was very close to them, and when he die they come ask me if I will help them when I'm in London, collect some information and pass it along."

"I see. And I was some of that information, right? Now, suddenly, I begin to get it. It wasn't any accident, your being in Paul's restaurant the other night. *You* thought I was a CIA man, too. You did, didn't you?"

Dumbly, she nodded.

"Jesus Christ!" She became the point on which all his

fury could gather. "You heard I'd seen Fitzhugh and you were told I was working with him on this Sung vase business. You were told to contact me again—I'll bet that's it. What a nitwit I was. I thought it was too good to be true, our getting together again. All you wanted was to find out what I was up to."

"No, Marius! You feel sorry for yourself, you make it all bad. It's not so. I didn't want see you again, but I was ordered to—all right. But when we have love affair last year, was nothing about Taiwan in it. And I don't stop loving you, not then, not this time either. Was very hard for me. You don't think about that." Her voice broke, and she began to cry.

It sobered him. He was no less shaken, but his anger was blunted, and with her tears, it faded. He pulled out a handkerchief and passed it to her.

"You can't expect me to take this lightly, Mei," he said. "You have to admit, you were lying to me."

"I admit. I tried to warn you. What could I do? They don't give me choice. And my heart say I want see you anyway, in spite everything."

He yearned to take her in his arms but he couldn't quite forgive her, not yet.

"So everything I told you yesterday was no news to you," he said. "You knew all about the theft. Everything you said was pretense, and lies. You even lied to me about Sun Chih-mo. You told me he was in the pay of the Reds, but I've found out he isn't. Why? What were you up to?"

She had dried her eyes, and still holding his handkerchief, she sat down. She seemed quite calm, a trifle flushed from the whisky. He understood, now, why she had needed it.

"All right," she said, "now you think. I told you I know Formosans didn't steal vase. But *whoever* stole, if it makes trouble for Communists, is good for us, so we must protect. You see that?"

"Yes, of course." He shrugged. "Just like the Russians. They were doing the same thing."

"*Yi ting*—certainly. As soon you tell me about what happened to you with Russians, I know they didn't take, and they trying to make you think they did to protect the real thief. Now, I know Mr. Sun not work for Formosa. But if he send you to see Russians, maybe it's because he knows who is thief. If he think you are CIA, and you looking for thief, he push you in wrong direction. When I think this, then I think I have to protect *him,* so I tell you lie about him. You must remember, I think you are CIA, too."

"I see," Marius said. "Everybody was covering up for everybody else, sending me running around in circles because they thought I'd get too close. Fitzhugh hinted as much to me. I should have paid more attention to him."

"That's why I wanted come to hotel tonight," Mei said, in a subdued voice. "I wanted search the room when you gone. When I heard you talking to that man tonight, I knew everybody mistaken, that you don't work for CIA. All right, I think it doesn't matter so much. Then you told me somebody tried to kill you." She sprang up, holding him by the arms, looking up at him in distress. "You in big danger. If they try once, they try again. I can't let you be killed. I don't care who took vase. That's why I tell you the truth now, so you know what going on, what you mixed up in. How you get away?"

Her fingers clutched painfully through the cloth of his jacket. "Stop it, Mei," he said, trying to sound calm. "I'll be all right." A thought struck him. "You're putting yourself in jeopardy by telling me, aren't you?"

"Never mind about me. Nobody bother about me.

You must go, leave London right away, tomorrow. If you go, nobody care to hurt you any more."

She shook at him, as if trying to make him move. He got his arms free and put them around her.

"Listen, will you?" he said. "I don't have to leave this minute. Good God, it must be nearly five o'clock. In the first place, I have to get some sleep. They're not going to try to knock me off in broad daylight, so I've got at least another day. And I don't want to run out now. I've been pushed around enough. I want to do a little pushing myself. Can you understand that?"

"No," she said, sadly. "I think you do too much."

"It wouldn't be—" he began, and bit off the rest of the sentence. He had been about to say, It wouldn't be that you want to get me out of the way before I can find out who the thief actually is? But looking into her eyes, full of concern, he knew that wasn't so—or at any rate, not altogether so. It was true that she loved him and didn't want him harmed. Her telling him the truth was evidence enough of that.

So he said, instead, "I have one more thing to find out. Then I can pass the whole business on to Fitzhugh. Come on, sit down for a minute."

He settled her in one of the armchairs. He brought the straight chair over, set it beside her, and sat down close enough so that he could put his hand on hers.

"Okay," he said. "Now that we're having some truth, what about Wang Lai? Do you know anything about him?"

"No, really, I don't know anything about."

"He's one of the keys. When he told me to meet him at three in the morning it was because he must already have had some idea that I'd have to be silenced. What about Sun Chih-mo, then? You said before that maybe he knew who the thief was, and that was why you had to steer me away from him. Why did you think that?"

She tucked her legs under her. "When you first talk to me about him, you told me he spends a lot of time at the museum, and he could know all about dustmen. I think right away, maybe he has something to do with thief, and he send you to Russians to cover up. I know Russians never come to him. What for? If they have vase, they not going sell it, they hide away. I'm sure he make that up to deceive you, send you—what they say?—chase after goose."

"But why? If he's not working with your people, whose side is he on?"

"There are other sides," she said, slowly, as if reluctant to go on. "Well, I mean, some old-time people who against Communists but not in favor of Formosa. Some rich people who left China, who liked the Republic but don't like Mao or Chiang Kai-shek. Do you know what is *Ko Lao Hui?*

With a forefinger, she traced the characters on the palm of her hand.

"I've heard of it, I think," Marius said. "The Society of Elder Brothers. Some kind of secret society, wasn't it?"

"A long time ago. First, was peasants, in early days of revolution. Even Sun Yat-sen belonged. Then it became composed rich businessmen, very reactionary."

"You're not saying it still exists and—?"

"No, I don't mean that. But China used to have many secret societies like that, some good, some bad, some just criminals."

"Like the *tongs,* in America."

"I suppose so. What I tell you is maybe still some secret societies here in Britain, people who go their own way, get together to fix up what's good for business. And if they want do something against the Reds, they do on their own hook."

"I see," said Marius. "Freelance operators. Then you think if there is such a secret society, Sun belongs to it?"

"I don't know. And again, there is another possibility. Mr. Sun is big dealer in Chinese art. Maybe he has customer who doesn't mind paying for something stolen from the Communists."

"In that case, Commander Wilde was right. But how would something like the Gow Yok Trading Company come into it?"

"They export as well as import—just like my company."

"And they could find a way of sending the vase out of the country to a customer who wasn't too particular."

Marius sat with his chin in his palm, thinking it over. At length, he said, "Fitzhugh told me that Sun was getting money from the Americans. How would that tie in? That CIA man told me they had orders to stay out of it."

Mei smiled, with a flash of her old self. "I don't know if it's true or not. But if it is, you never heard how mandarins in old days take with two hands, one in front and one behind?"

Marius stood up and pulled his necktie loose. "I'm beat," he said. "I haven't had so much exercise since I played shortstop for Pratt's Falls High."

"But what you going to do?" asked Mei.

"Get some sleep."

"Now, Marius, don't joke. Is not funny."

"No kidding?" He unbuttoned his shirt and went into the bedroom. She followed him, climbing into the bed and resting her arms on her updrawn knees.

"I'm going to report everything so far to Fitzhugh,"

Marius said, yawning. "At least, I know one thing for sure that he doesn't—the Russians haven't got it. Before I see him, I want to try to track down whoever owns that Gow Yok company. Then I'll have a nice, neat package to hand Fitzhugh. I'm looking forward to seeing his face when I tell him." He kicked off his shoes, and sat on the bed to take his socks off, groaning. "Who do I know in the catering business who might be able to help?" He paused, raising a finger, "Paul Li! Of course! I wonder if he'd tell me anything."

Mei opened her mouth and closed it again. A kind of comic flash, not quite a smile, passed across her face. Then she said, "I think he will, if you ask it him in right way."

He squinted at her. "Why do you say it like that? You've got that smug look on your face—what do you mean, 'the right way'?"

"If you tell him you a CIA man."

"Mei! Don't tell me Paul is somehow tied up in this thing, too!"

"Not exactly, not like me. But his restaurant used by the Communists to listen what going on, and also for meeting place for their agents. He's very useful to them, and so they pay for restaurant."

"Paul? Paul is working for the Reds? Oh, well," said Marius, tossing his trousers on a chair, "nothing ought to surprise me any more." He began laughing, rather weakly. "So if Paul is on their payroll, he'll help me. Naturally. They'd like the thief to be found, but they aren't going to do anything directly, themselves. It's the job of the British and I suppose the Chinese are waiting to see whether they can do it."

He crawled into bed, snuggling close to Mei, who took him in her arms.

"Okay," he whispered. "Tomorrow I'll talk to Paul. After that I'll see Fitzhugh. And then I'll catch the first plane for Paris. And you can come or not, whatever you like."

He felt her hands, cool on his back, sliding down his ribs. Confused images shifted in his mind: Mei saying the Chinese had no concept of Original Sin, Sun Chih-mo smiling fatly, Wang Lai full of gratitude, and Chinese vases and pots and bowls of a dazzling purity of glaze and color. The thought he had had earlier in the day, it seemed years ago, that everyone was playing a part, that he was surrounded by false faces, by deception, came surging back. Whom can you trust? he thought, and felt himself sliding, sliding, into the safety of sleep.

Chapter 11

He opened his eyes out of a rambling monologue of dream, his mouth dry and foul-tasting, the smell of his own body abhorrent, his arms and neck aching as if he had lain tensely for hours instead of sleeping. He sat up. A rod of dusty sunlight probed through the drawn curtains, and he saw that there was a note on the bed table, weighted down by his watch.

He looked at the time: ten-thirty. He picked up the note, knowing what it would say. *I did not want to waken you, you were so tired, & I did not want breakfast, I have some appointments this morning, please take care, ring me, please be careful.*

He got out of bed, creasing the note between his fingers and tearing it across and across. He understood her delicacy, she hadn't wanted to appear downstairs with him. And maybe it was something more. Another woman might have needed to justify herself, might have required more talk to explain her duplicity, but in Mei's case he knew there was a difference: she wouldn't want him to have to face her this morning. She had given him time to think.

Please be careful, he muttered, going to draw a bath. Yes, but of whom? He was like a man wandering in an exotic wood—"Don't touch that, it's poisonous," "That lizard is venomous"—and now he had to add Mei to the list, didn't he? "That butterfly is lovely but it stings." Oh, Christ! he thought, if only I could say the hell with her, if only I didn't care about her.

Bathed, shaved, dressed, throwing the windows wide to the warm, dusty air, he looked down at the street and only after a moment realized that he had been unconsciously searching for his shadowers. "There must be dozens of you out there now," he said. "Where the hell are you?" And there might be one sent from whoever had tried to kill him the night before, watching for another chance, lurking in a phone booth with a poisoned butterfly trained to flutter over dealers in Oriental art.

In the broad light of day, he couldn't believe it and he began to chuckle. It was all too fantastic, Marius Kagan, that nice, respectable man, fifty-two years old, a bachelor, without an enemy in the world except for business rivals, well-liked, welcomed everywhere, that Marius Kagan whose arena was the sale room and whose field was porcelain—porcelain, my God!—and Chinese landscapes and bronze ritual vessels, that Marius mixed up in international espionage, violence, theft, and attempted murder? Impossible! The motorcyclist must have been stoned out of his wits and it had been an accident magnified into a conspiracy by the lateness of the hour; a drunk fumbling around in the wrong hotel room had been imagined to be a CIA agent. His heart sank. It was no good trying to pretend. It was all, unfortunately, true.

He got out his address book and looked up Paul Li's number. While it was ringing he considered what to say. He had become more cautious.

"Mustard Seed Garden, Paul Li speaking."

"Hello, Paul. It's Marius. I want to see you. It's urgent."

"Yes, Marius, what's it about? I'm rather busy."

"You know that Chu Ta album leaf? I've got to sell it in a hurry. If you want it, you can have it very cheaply. But I have to make the deal right away."

He could almost feel the other's puzzlement over the wire.

"Fine," Li said, at last. "Why don't you come for lunch?"

"No, I'd rather not discuss business in public. Can't I come over right now?"

"Of course, if you'd rather."

"I'd rather."

When he had hung up, he sat for a few minutes with his hand on the phone, hesitating over calling Mei. He no longer felt so biting a sense of outrage; she had, after all, thrown off her dissimulation because of her concern for him. What troubled him was that since she had been part of the general deceit around him, he no longer knew how far he could trust her. Behind that mask might be other masks—how did he know, for instance, that her apparent candor now did not conceal some other purpose? You could play that game inside yourself endlessly, in which you saw truth used only as another species of lie. Once betrayed, you could go on imagining levels of betrayal too deep to fathom.

He shrugged the feeling off. In spite of everything, he had to see her again if for nothing else but to reopen the wound, to take revenge, perhaps, or simply to say goodbye. Love, he told himself bitterly, lifting the receiver, turned out to be less simple when you grew older.

Mei's voice was businesslike and impersonal. "You feel better now you had some sleep?"

"Yes, I feel fine. What's your program for the day?"

"My program?"

"I thought we ought to see each other. I'm going to Paris."

"Now? You're going now?"

"No, I'm going to see Paul in a little while. Then I have a couple of other things to wrap up. I thought I'd take the plane late this afternoon."

She was silent so long that he said, "Hello?"

"I'm here. I was thinking. Are you angry?"

"No. I just have a lot on my mind."

"Shall we have dinner? If you come my flat—"

He had told her, last night, that he was leaving and that she could come with him or not, just as she chose. She had obviously chosen. He began to say no, and then shrugged. After all, there was a plane almost every hour. "All right," he said. "But make it early."

"Six o'clock?"

"Fine." And then, without intending to, he said in an altered voice, "Don't worry, honey. I'll be all right."

"Please," she said, softly. "Good-bye."

He remembered that he hadn't yet had any breakfast, but there was one more call to make, to Fitzhugh.

As before, the man who answered only said, "Yes?"

"This is Marius Kagan. I want to talk to Mr. Fitzhugh."

"Sorry, guv'nor, he's out. Any message?"

"I've got to see him, it's important. When will he be in?"

"Can't say. He'll be in touch with me, though."

"All right, tell him I'll ring back at one. Tell him I have some information for him, and I want to see him no later than about five. After that," Marius finished, with a satisfying sense of being in command, "he'll have to come to Paris to talk to me."

"Right-o, sir."

Marius took his briefcase and went downstairs. It was

nearly eleven-thirty and he'd have to hurry, for he didn't want to phone Fitzhugh from Li's restaurant. Reluctantly, he gave up the idea of breakfast and let the hall porter get him a taxi.

The head waiter at the Mustard Seed Garden knew him, and showed him to the private stair that led to Li's office. It was half a business office, with files and records and an efficient-looking desk, half a sitting room with a couple of comfortable Swedish armchairs and a low table near the front windows, a few good Chinese paintings on the walls, and shelves on which were some fine pieces of bronze, pottery and jade. Li opened the door to his knock and shook hands, drawing him into the room.

"Paul, you can save my life if you want to," Marius said.

"What—?"

"I've got to have a cup of coffee."

Even as the words were out, he saw the abrupt change in Li's expression and was shocked into the realization that the other already knew something about what was going on, and, in the same breath, that it was no joking matter.

"Of course," Li said, recovering his poise at once.

He switched on his intercom and called down for coffee and biscuits, while Marius dropped into one of the armchairs, wondering how to begin. He opened his case and slowly brought out the painting.

"Ah, lovely," said Li.

He rolled up a small picture of chrysanthemums by Wang Yi-t'ing which Marius had once sold him and hung the Chu Ta in its place. "It is a gem," he said, bending forward to look more closely at the brushwork.

A waiter arrived with a tray, and for a few minutes Marius was totally absorbed in swallowing his coffee and hungrily crunching up five or six dryish sugared biscuits.

Then Li, sitting down, said, "This was very quick, wasn't it? I mean, your decision to sell it."

Marius understood the gambit. Paul thought he needed money in a hurry for something and was preparing to drive as hard a bargain as he could.

"Actually," he began, and stopped, for once at a loss. Whatever happened with the present affair, he was still a dealer, and Li was not only an old friend but a good customer. It wouldn't do to hold out a tidbit like the Chu Ta and then pull it back again.

"You really want it, don't you, Paul?" he said. "Okay, you can have it for fourteen hundred pounds. You know what I paid for it. I can sell it for twice that in the States."

Li nodded.

"I want a favor in return," Marius said.

"A favor? I can't imagine what I can do for you, Marius, but of course if it's possible—"

"Do you know a firm called the Gow Yok Trading Company?"

There was no perceptible alteration in Li's handsome, attentive features, but the air around him seemed to congeal into watchfulness.

"Well?" Marius said. "Do you or don't you?"

"Yes, I know it."

"Who owns it?"

Li removed his glasses and held them up to the light. He took out a silk handkerchief and polished them, and put them on again.

"Marius," he said, with deliberation, "I hope you'll forgive me for being blunt, but why, exactly, do you want to know?"

Marius drew a long breath. "All right," he said, "I'll tell you. I belong to a certain organization—er—" He tried frantically to remember what he had read about the CIA that would give him an air of authenticity. "We call it the Company. And I'm on the trail of—that is, I've been assigned to the case of a certain missing object. I'm sure I don't have to go into more detail with you, Paul. You see, I know where *you* stand." And, he added to himself, I hope Mei was right about you, old buddy, otherwise I don't know what comes next.

But he needn't have worried. Paul nodded, smiling, and said, "I thought as much. I had the tip that you'd been dealing with a certain British agent, and that you were in Central Intelligence. You needn't be so mysterious—but then, I know your people love that sort of thing. Right. You understand, I can't be openly involved in anything. But I don't mind giving you some information in this case, since we're on the same side. So you've run the thing down to a connection with Gow Yok? That's very interesting. That company is owned by Sun Chih-mo."

Marius sank back in his chair, shoving his hands into his jacket pockets. He had thought nothing would surprise him, and indeed, he was beyond further shock. He said, quite evenly, "Is that so? But he works for the—I mean, for *us,* doesn't he?"

"If you say so," Li replied, with delicate courtesy. "You asked me for some information, Marius, and I've given it to you."

Marius mulled it over. It all fitted together, of course. He had long ago pointed out that Sun was in a good position to find out the name of the contractor who collected the museum's rubbish, and the days on which the truck would come. Nothing would have been easier for him than to organize the whole deal, using a truck from his own company. Naturally, then, if he had been behind the robbery, he would have steered Marius away to the Russians, particularly if he had thought Marius worked with the CIA and was on the track of the vase. Even Wang Lai's double-dealing could be traced to Sun, for nothing was more probable than that the small dealer should know the big one. Sun might even have some hold on the other, perhaps something to do with the mah-jong parlor. If Sun secretly owned a trading company, who knew what other pies he might have fingers in?

And why would he have done it? Aram Tashjian had said, *There's always a buyer for everything.* A man with Sun's connections might well have a buyer for a vase of this quality and rarity. It would surely pay enough to make any risk worthwhile. If that were so, they might as well kiss the vase good-bye, for it was probably on its way out of the country by now.

He said, with a sigh, "Thanks, Paul. That's it, I guess. Oh, one other thing—do you know a man named Wang Lai?"

"*Ta hao jên Wang?*—Good-natured Wang? Everyone knows him. The one with the shop in Lisle Street with a gambling parlor in the cellar, is that the man?"

"Yes. I'm just trying to think what possible connection there could be between him and Sun."

Li said, "Ah. I see." He said it in a strange, tight voice, which made Marius stare at him.

"What do you see?" Marius asked.

Li got up and went to the door. He opened it a little way and peered out. Then he walked to a window and stood looking down into the street.

He said, "Tell me something. Just how close to it are you?"

"How close? What do you mean?"

"These questions, about the Gow Yok Company and Wang Lai—I presume you have a good idea who has the Sung vase. You're not just making a stab in the dark."

"I don't see how I can be wrong," Marius replied. "Sun organized the job, hired men from Ireland to pose as dustmen, used one of the Gow Yok trucks—I've seen it myself, with the name of the garbage collector painted out. Wang Lai owes me a favor, and when I asked him whether he knew of a Chinese company which had a small truck and might have hired some Irishmen, he told me to meet him on a street corner at three in the morning. When I got there, somebody on a motorcycle tried to run me down."

"When was this?"

"This morning. It's obvious there's some kind of a link between Wang and Sun, because the word about my snooping must have passed between them. Whether there is or not, Sun arranged for the vase to be stolen and I suppose he's sent it off to some rich collector in Singapore or some place, who will take it out to fondle every once in a while."

Li shook his head. "I don't think so. Until you asked about Wang, I might have agreed. As it is, I'm sure the vase is in London. I imagine that sooner or later a ransom will be asked for it. You might say it is being held hostage." He grinned, crookedly. "That's the fashionable thing these days, isn't it?"

Marius stood up. "Come on, Paul. Don't play the inscrutable Oriental. What are you talking about?"

"You've got to keep my name out of it."

"Absolutely."

"Wang Lai and Sun do have something in common," Li said, lowering his voice. "They both belong to the same society—*Shih P'ang.*"

"The Stone Circle? What does that mean?"

Li patted the air with a palm, saying, "Softly, softly, please. *Shih P'ang* is a fraternal organization. Have you ever heard of the Society of Elder Brothers, or the Green Circle headed by Tu Yu-sung?"

Marius suddenly recalled the last of his talk with Mei, just before he went to sleep. He had been too tired, then, and had all but forgotten what she had said, almost the same words, *Do you know what is* Ko Lao Hui?

"Secret societies?" he said. "What—you mean, like the Mafia?"

"No, no. Not criminals—I should say, not altogether," he amended. "Some of the societies in the old days were sometimes linked with criminal activities. The Green Circle wasn't above a spot of kidnapping, and the Red Circle in Canton did a lot of smuggling. But they were essentially businessmen's organizations, just as the Elder Brothers was a peasants' and farmers' society. Chairman Mao put an end to all of them, at least as far as the People's Republic is concerned. Some branches may have continued in Hong Kong and in other places.

"The Stone Circle is an association of—well, let's say like-minded people, people living here, who have banded together to set certain standards for business practices, to protect themselves from exploitation, to see to it that Western groups—like the Mafia, for instance—don't penetrate the Chinese community. You might say, they are a sort of Rotary Club."

Marius lifted an eyebrow, drawing down the corners of his mouth. "You're kidding," he said. "You mean they're neighborhood racketeers."

"That's unnecessarily crude," Li said, primly. "They think of themselves as merchants surrounded by hostile foreigners. They are a self-defense league. As far as I know—and I'm not a member, mind you, primarily because of my—ah—connections with—"

"Yes, I know. You needn't be so mysterious," Marius couldn't resist saying.

"Mhm. As far as I know, they try to keep clear of anything illegal unless they're driven to it out of desperation. Like all Chinese, they are clannish and patriotic. Unfortunately, from my point of view at least, their patriotism doesn't extend to the government of mainland China. So, although they are not all supporters of the Formosan regime, if they saw the chance of doing something which would harm the People's Republic, I'm afraid they'd take it. Or, let me put it this way, some of them would. Sun certainly would, he hates the Communists. The rest of the Circle might not go completely along with him, but they would be bound to give him their help if he asked for it."

"I see," Marius said. "And when Sun saw a chance of getting the vase, he couldn't resist it."

"Just so. I may say, it's a bit of a jolt," said Li. "Until you told me, today, I was certain it was the work of Formosan agents. I even thought your friend, Mrs. Yuan, had turned, for your sake, and was helping you. You know all about her, I assume. I imagine some other people have thought so, too."

Marius stiffened. "What other people?"

"Surely I needn't go into details," Li replied. "I'd have thought she had already taken that into account. Hasn't she?"

"Oh, sure. I suppose she has." Marius shifted uneasily, not wanting to sound ignorant because of what he was supposed to be, but wishing Paul would be plainer.

"But of course, it's none of my business," Li went on, cheerily. "I'm only an observer. Please remember that.

In any case, I know that my people will be glad to know who has the vase even though getting it back may be something of a problem. I must admit," he added, with an amused, sidelong glance at Marius, "that I wonder a little at finding your organization taking an interest in the matter. It seems to indicate a new orientation, doesn't it?"

"I'd rather you didn't talk about it," Marius said, with a sinking at the stomach. All he needed now was for the whole balance of power in the world to be reshuffled just because he was posing as a CIA man. "You understand, Paul—it's got to be kept very quiet."

"Certainly, I understand. I'm sure there's more to it than meets the eye."

"You can say that again," Marius said, fervently. "Anyway, my part's finished. I'll be leaving London shortly." He held out a hand. "Thanks a lot. I appreciate it."

Li shook hands with him, and said, "I'm the one who is grateful. I'll just write you out a check."

"A check? What for?"

"Fourteen hundred pounds," Li said, sounding bewildered. "Isn't that right?"

"Ah, well," Marius sighed. "It shows you what a state I'm in. I never thought the day would come when I'd forget a sale."

After leaving Li, Marius phoned Fitzhugh again from a kiosk. He was told by the man who answered that he could come at five. He returned to the Comus, had a good lunch, packed his bag, left it with the hall porter, and settled his bill. He made some business phone calls, feeling that with them he was returning to the world of sanity. With a comfortable couple of hours to kill, he strolled to Bond Street and toured a few galleries: a show of paintings of newspaper headlines, meticulously copied even to the ink smudges; an exhibition of plastic sculpture shaped like turds; a group show of the work of four members of a Devon commune whose manifesto was that Art must be Edible. Marius told himself not to be a snob, for after all Chinese painting might be as incomprehensible to most people as this stuff was to him.

At five sharp, he was knocking at the door of Electrodyne Research Co. But this time, there was a difference, he felt curiously exhilarated and on top of things. When the door was opened for him by the man with the beaky nose and bulging forehead, he said, "Hey, how come you're not following me?"

The other only grinned, and said, "This way, sir."

He ushered Marius into the back room, where Fitzhugh was working at some papers at the table. He pushed them away and got up, motioning to a chair.

"Well, Mr. Kagan," he said, with a touch of irritability, "you were very insistent. Is it really important?"

Marius very deliberately settled himself in the armchair and put his briefcase on the floor. "I wouldn't mind a drink," he said. "Got any whisky?"

"I'm afraid not," Fitzhugh said, flushing slightly and keeping his eyes away from the chest of drawers. "Look here, I'm really fearfully busy—"

"So am I," Marius retorted. "And your Goddamned little caper has screwed up *my* life and *my* business. I've had about enough of it. But I know who's got the vase."

Fitzhugh's start was perceptible. Marius, studying him with an eye sharpened by years of experience as a dealer, was satisfied to see that he had lost his composure. Very nice, he told himself. That's stopped the bidding, hasn't it?

Fitzhugh sat down, at last, and said, "I find it very

difficult—" He stopped, and then began again. "Suppose you tell me what you think you've found."

Marius settled back, saying within himself, I am not going to take any shit from you. Aloud, he said, "Slight correction. Not what I *think* I've found; what I've *found.* The vase was stolen by somebody hired by a secret society called *Shih P'ang,* or as you would say, not knowing any Chinese, the Stone Circle. Mr. Sun Chih-mo is a member. He has been working with the director of the Adjai, and so he was able to find out the name of the contractor who picked up the museum's rubbish and the dates of the collections. The truck that was used belongs to him. Okay? How's that—detailed enough for you?"

Fitzhugh was speechless. Marius crossed his legs, meticulously hitching up his trousers. "That's why Sun sent me off after the Russians," he continued, enjoying himself. "Another member of the society tried to have me knocked off by a motorcyclist last night, because I was getting too close to the truth."

"Last night—?"

"That's it. I'm not going to go into everything else that's happened, but I've had enough. More than enough, too fucking much if you'll forgive my emotional language."

Fitzhugh barely heard him. He was having trouble masking his consternation so that it would look like nothing more than the astonishment he might be expected to feel.

This was the last thing he had looked for. He had begun the whole affair with this Kagan fellow as a diversion. It had looked so simple and so neat. By appearing to be working with an American agent he would cover his own attempts to protect whoever the thief was. At the same time, the participation of a CIA man would seem to point at the Russians, the best diversion of all since of course he knew they had *not* stolen the vase. He had been reminded of his Kipling, "the bleating of the kid . . ." Kagan would serve as a lure to which, perhaps, the tiger would come, designed to keep everyone's attention—including Commander Wilde's—off Fitzhugh and perhaps, at the same time, off the real thief. There had always been the possibility that Kagan might be killed; that would have been supportable. On the other hand, there had also been the chance that he might turn up some interesting bit of information so that Fitzhugh could fulfill his main task, which was the concealment of the thief, since any blow against Red China was precisely what his employers wanted.

And now, the wretched little sod had torn it. The question was, what was to come next?

He said, as heartily as he could, "Mr. Kagan, if I seem stunned it's because you have managed something neither my department nor the police have been able to do. I don't mind telling you, I'm impressed."

Marius would have been less than human if he had been able to keep from smiling.

Fitzhugh lit a cheroot, eyeing him through the smoke. It was important to try to find out who else might know, who might have given Kagan the tip, who stood on which side. On the table, among his papers, were the reports from the man he had assigned to follow Kagan. Among the people who had been in touch with him, there was at least one so far unidentified.

He went on, "Would you like to tell me how you found out?"

His attitude had been so flattering that, almost, Marius blurted everything out. But he was able to catch himself; he couldn't mention Mei's part, nor that of Paul Li.

"Sorry," he said, "I'm afraid I can't. The people who helped me did so in confidence. You'll just have to take my word for it that it's a fact. I can tell you that I myself saw the truck that was used. That was last night, when I was trying to get away from the motorcyclist—that was a fact, too."

"I see. It would be better, of course, if you could give me a few more leads, something a bit more specific. Where is the vase now?"

"That's something I don't know, except that it's probably in London. I heard—well, it's obvious that the Stone Circle is going to have it handy so that they can use it as a—a hostage. They'll use it to bargain with, I should think. Anyway, that's another thing I wanted to tell you. You wanted me to help you identify the vase when you found it. You'll have to get someone else, because I'm leaving. I'm going to Paris tonight."

"Oh?"

"I'm not interested in getting killed, so don't try to stop me."

Fitzhugh blew out a long plume of smoke, in relief. He wanted nothing more than to get Marius out of London and as far away as possible.

"I wouldn't dream of stopping you," he said. "I'll manage somehow."

"You might get Simon Metcalfe of the Beauvoir Collection. He's got all the qualifications. I don't know why you didn't pick him in the first place."

"Yes, yes." Fitzhugh waved a hand. "I—ah—considered him. Don't trouble yourself about it. With that society—the Stone Circle?—knowing about you, you could be in grave danger. On the whole, I think I'd have to urge you to leave if you hadn't already decided on it yourself. By the by, have you told anyone else about this?"

"Nobody."

"Good. After all, we don't want you harmed, do we?"

"No, we don't. Which reminds me. That guy you have tailing me—"

"Thomas? Yes, an efficient man."

"I don't know how efficient he is. I shook him last night. I suppose he has to sleep some time. Anyway, I sort of wished I hadn't been so smart, later, because maybe if he'd been around we might have nailed the man who tried to run me down. Do you think—?"

"I'll keep him after you until you get on the airplane," Fitzhugh said, feeling positively amicable. Things couldn't have worked out better.

He glanced at his notes. "Splendid," he said. "Far more than I expected. You've really been an immense help. Now, just to wind up one or two details . . . you don't mind, do you?"

"I don't know whether I do or not. What do you mean by one or two details?"

"Someone came to visit you at your hotel yesterday morning at about nine-thirty. He is described as a man of medium height, portly build, about middle age, long hair and beard, wearing a tweed jacket, looks vaguely Central European. Who would that have been?"

"You people really are thorough, aren't you?" Marius said, admiringly. "How do I know who— Oh, yes. I remember. It was a customer. In fact, now I think of it, he said he was a friend of yours. He gave you as a reference."

Fitzhugh looked at him blankly. "Me? What's his name?"

"Guy Neuville."

A brief pulsation of dizziness, a kind of acrophobic vertigo, passed through Fitzhugh's head. In all the nervous, painful, slippery years of his service as a double agent he had had many alarums, but he had never had a short half hour so crammed with shock as this one. He inspected Marius with loathing, thinking how pleasant it would be to push him under the slicing wheels of a locomotive. He pulled himself together.

"How on earth did you meet him?" he asked.

"In a restaurant. He was with some Chinese man, and introduced himself to me, said he was interested in Chinese art and knew my name. He came to the hotel and I showed him some things. He's a real screwball, isn't he?"

"Yes, you could call him that," Fitzhugh said, abstractedly. "I didn't actually know he knew anything about Chinese art."

"I don't think he knows much. Is he always like that —I mean, rambling on, talking in a confused sort of way? He kept telling me he wanted to get a job in America."

"Yes, he's very odd," Fitzhugh replied. Everything had suddenly become clear. He added, warily, "Did he —what did he say about me?"

"He said he could tell me some embarrassing things about you," Marius chuckled. "Maybe I ought to pump him. What'd you do, go to school together?"

"No, we didn't. My advice to you is to stay away from Neuville. Don't have anything further to do with him. He hasn't any money and preys on his friends, or on anyone gullible enough to listen to him."

"I don't think of myself as gullible."

"I didn't mean that, exactly."

"Funny he'd give your name as a reference, then, isn't it?"

"Not at all. I told you he was odd. We were once good friends, and he has borrowed money from me in the past. However, as long as you're leaving London there's no harm done. What time are you leaving, by the way?"

"I have a dinner date, and then there's a plane around eleven. I'll probably take that."

"Good," said Fitzhugh, adding, under his breath, "riddance."

For some time after Marius had gone, he sat on looking out the windows at the gloomy courtyard. He could see where he was being driven, and the prospect filled him with dread, starting the cold sweat trickling down his ribs. He had once before had to kill a man, nearly ten years ago, and had almost bungled it. He had been bolder then, too, and less hag-ridden by drink and the fear of exposure. But he could see no way out of this except murder.

It was obvious that Guy could no longer be trusted in the slightest. The word which Fitzhugh had cautiously circulated, that Marius was a CIA agent, must somehow, God knew how, have reached Neuville's ears. He was, therefore, playing both ends, fishing for a job with the Americans, while working for Fitzhugh and the Russians. That phrase "some embarrassing things" sent a shudder through him. If Kagan had been a real Central Intelligence agent he'd have jumped at it, would have known at once what it meant. And how long would it be before Neuville decided that there was more money to be had out of the Chinese than the trifle Fitzhugh had doled out to him, hard-earned money which he had dug out of his own pocket? Once Kagan left London, Neuville would consider that chance gone, and then it was only a matter of time.

Not much time, either. Guy had already made contact with the Chinese, following Fitzhugh's orders to find out more about what they wanted. He could see, now, that that had been a mistake; he had taken that course in the hope of postponing more drastic action, but now it wouldn't be long before the Chinese began pressing

Neuville. It would end in blackmail, or worse. He had tried not to see how shaky Guy really was, but he couldn't shut his eyes to it any longer.

So it had better be at once, before he lost his nerve. He jumped up and pulled open the bureau drawer. After he had had a stiff one, not bothering with a glass, he reached into the back of the drawer and got out the Browning in its flat holster. His hands had become very cold and he had to master their trembling. He made sure there was a full clip, and snapped back the slide to load the chamber. Then he left the office without a word, to find a public telephone kiosk.

Chapter 12

For a time, after he left the Electrodyne office, all Marius's attention was directed to getting a taxi in the evening rush, but on the way to Mei's, at last, he was able to remember the end of his conversation with Fitzhugh and to recall, as well, that Neuville had taken the jade bear and left him £25. So much had happened that that minor incident had gone out of his head altogether. It was, he told himself, a blasted nuisance. It irked him to leave a piece of unfinished business, especially when he had already taken some money and the customer was holding an item worth eight times as much.

He fumbled around in his pockets and finally found the piece of paper on which Neuville had written his address and phone number, remembering as well that he had agreed to visit the man—when? His sense of time was muddled; my God! he thought, it was yesterday morning he visited me, that means our appointment was for tonight. After eleven, the fellow had said. Well, that wouldn't do, not if he wanted to make the eleven o'clock plane.

Mei was wearing a *ch'i pao* of dark gray silk, like the plumage of a ringdove, fastened up to the neck with spinach jade buttons. She looked so soft and demure that the idea of her being a secret agent was preposterous. He kissed her and said, "I have to make a phone call. Let me just get business out of the way."

He dialed Neuville's number, biting his lip, willing the man to be in. He was almost ready to hang up, when the voice said, "Hello?"

"Mr. Neuville? This is Marius Kagan."

There was a brief silence, then, "Mario who?"

"Kagan (you idiot, he almost added). This is Mr. Neuville, isn't it?"

"Oh—I beg your pardon. Mr. Kagan. Yes, of course." And then, unaccountably, he began to laugh.

"We were supposed to get together tonight," Marius said, petulantly.

"Yes, I know. Sorry. I'm really terribly sorry. I've just had another phone call from someone else, a mutual friend, and it struck me as funny. Yes, of course, Mr. Kagan. You were coming here at eleven, weren't you?"

"I was," Marius said, somewhat mollified, "but I'm going to have to leave London tonight and that'll be too late. Can I come earlier?"

"What time would you like to make it?"

Marius glanced at Mei, and tried to calculate. Half an hour to the airport, by cab, and he had to pick up his luggage at the Comus before that. The business with Neuville shouldn't take more than a quarter of an hour. Still, he ought to leave a little leeway. "Say, nine-thirty?"

"That'll be all right. My other guest should be gone by then."

As Marius hung up, Mei, who had been watching him, said, "You are really going."

He nodded.

"I see," she said. It was hardly more than a sigh.

She had set a small table near the french window, covered with a cloth, lighted by a three-branched candlestick, laid with eggshell bowls and spoons and lacquered chopsticks. She lighted the candles and said, "Come, sit down. I have some things you like."

There were prawns with ginger, duck pancakes, lemon chicken, but he hadn't much appetite. He forced himself to eat, and drank several glasses of wine. They spoke casually, almost coolly, about inconsequential things, until at last Marius put down his chopsticks.

"What's the use?" he said. "We may as well talk about it."

"I don't know what else to say, only good-bye." She did not look at him.

"Mei, you must know how I feel. You played a double game with me. You can't blame me for being unsure of you." He hadn't meant to start this way, but out it came.

She raised her eyes. "If I don't blame you, why you blame me? I have a job to do. Is not my fault. Oh!" she cried, throwing down her napkin and rising so abruptly that the chair fell over. "You are—" She couldn't find the word she wanted and continued in Chinese, "What did you come here for? You say that you love me, but you do nothing but torment me. When I knew you were in real danger I told you everything, I did what I could to help you. How can we be together if you will always look at me so suspiciously? What do you want of me? Why don't you go?"

She had spoken so rapidly and with such passion that he could barely follow what she said. He jumped up, too, and caught her by the arms above the elbows, almost shaking her.

"Listen!" he said. "I'm not blaming you. Just try to see it my way. From the start—from the very beginning when I got mixed up in this shit—nothing has been the way it looked. Everybody has worn a mask, everybody!

Sun Chih-mo isn't just a respectable art dealer, the Russians were pretending, little Mr. Wang—the man I thought owed me a favor—tried to have me murdered. At the start, I was even wrong about the man who was following me. Then a tourist I kept meeting turned out to be a secret agent. Even the man who first got me involved in the case started out as a nebbish with a wine jar to sell and turned out to be a British agent. And Paul, he was masquerading, too."

He let go of her, his shoulders slumping. He searched her face as if he could stare her into understanding. "And you," he said. "That was the biggest shock of all, Mei. I know it wasn't your fault, but I found I was floating around in lies and I still don't know what the real truth is about anything. I feel I've been used by everybody for their own purposes. It's that kind of a world—a world in which ordinary people can suddenly find themselves being used as hostages, held like pieces of property for investment, swapped around for somebody's advantage like those little houses in a Monopoly game. The Sung vase, for instance. It's just a piece in the game, not a work of art—"

He stopped, for unaccountably, into his mind had come the vision of the sale room, of his bidding against Claudel for a Japanese screen, of his using that work of art first for revenge and then to pay off his debt to Nakamura. He uttered a bitter laugh.

"I'm not much different," he said. "How can I blame you? I was going around wearing my own mask, although I didn't know it. You thought I was working for the CIA."

She came close, reaching up to hold his face between her palms.

"Don't be angry," she said.

"I'm not," he said, slipping his arms around her. "Do

you know what I want? I want you to make up your mind and come with me to Paris. And after that, to New York. Let's leave it all behind, Mei. Let's get married, anything you like, so long as we're together. I've had it, up to here. It's you I want. Well, what about it? Or do you want me to say it in Chinese?"

"No, I understand," she said, smiling.

"What do you say?"

"You really want me?"

"You know I do."

"All right."

She said it so simply that it took a moment for it to sink in. "You mean it?" he said.

She nodded, and he kissed her.

"I can't do right away," she said, when they had drawn apart again. "I can't come tonight, I have some things to do. You ring me from Paris and I meet you there. I have to make arrangements about my business. All right?"

"All right? Sure it's all right. I can't believe it. Listen, I'm sure things will work out," he babbled. "There's no reason you can't manage your business from New York. We could come over here every month. Maybe Richard could go to some American university." He hugged her to him. "I know we can work it out. I just wish you could come with me tonight. I have to see this guy about a piece of jade he wants to buy, and I had figured on taking the eleven o'clock plane, but there are lots of planes. Or I could come back here and stay over, and we could go tomorrow morning. How about that?"

She chuckled. "You are like schoolboy."

"I feel like a kid."

"But we not children, Marius, we can wait a bit longer. You ring me tomorrow night and tell me where you are. I make sure to be ready then and I join you."

"I'm just afraid of losing you. Maybe you'll change your mind."

"I won't change my mind," she answered, lifting her lips to his.

After he had gone, she remained standing before the door, resting her forehead against the smooth, cool panel. She did love him, very much, but she could never tell him the plain truth, which was that she *had* to leave London. Only an hour before Marius had arrived, her chief, Mr. Feng, had paid her a visit. He was very angry, indeed, for it began to be clear that she had not carried out her assignment; word had reached him that the American had already discovered more than was good for him, and far from heading him off she appeared to be helping him. Under the circumstances, she was of no further use as an agent. She should be grateful, he pointed out, coldly, that she had not been employed by the other side, for the fate of unsuccessful agents there was more dismal than a mere discharge. He could not, he added, guarantee her safety in any event, since whoever had stolen the vase might now be thinking of retaliation. He would do what he could to protect her for a day or two, but his advice was that it might be best for everyone concerned if she were to leave the country within twenty-four hours, and stay away until things had had a chance to blow over.

Even so, she thought, going slowly to clear the table, her words to Marius had not been lies, for she did love him. No doubt she would manage in America, although her whole being resisted the idea of uprooting herself again and living among strangers. It would be better, for her peace of mind as well as his, that none of this ever became an issue between them. Far better to let him think that it was her desire, alone, that made her go with him.

Marius's euphoria was still with him in the taxi, on the way to Neuville's. He kept turning over plans, considering how to rearrange the house to make the small guest bedroom into an office for Mei, and maybe enlarge the master bedroom so as to have more closet space. He opened both windows of the cab to cool his face, and looked out at the dusky buildings, blue with evening, gold-spangled with windows, feeling gratitude to London for being the place where he had met her. The taxi turned off the Edgware Road, and on the corner a newspaper seller's placards shouted their customary tale of ruin and disaster: SOHO RESTAURANT BOMB—TWO HURT; it seemed no more than an accent to the pure happiness that filled him. The cab stopped before a high, narrow brick house in a darkish little side street, and he got out, too preoccupied to do more than wonder in passing that a man who could spend £200 on a piece of jade should live in such a neighborhood. There was no accounting for eccentricity.

He held out a pound note to the driver. "I'll be here for about fifteen minutes," he said, "and then I have to go to the Comus Hotel and then out to the airport. Do you want to wait for me?"

"Righty-ho, sir."

There were five bells with names beside them, and Marius had to borrow some matches from the cabdriver so that he could see them. The topmost one said, *Flat 5, Neuville,* and he pressed the bell and waited, but nothing happened. He tried the door; it was unlocked.

Flat 5 was on the top floor and he was puffing a little when he got there. He surveyed the scratched door with distaste, and knocked. To his astonishment, it moved under his fist, opening a crack. He pushed at it tentatively, saying, "Hello?"

There was a kind of scrabbling noise inside, like a dog trying to dig up a floor.

Marius stood undecided. "Hello," he said, again, and at length thought he might as well just look inside, although he had begun to feel some misgiving.

The room was lighted by a brass-stemmed floor lamp with a fringed shade like a hat out of some Oriental pageant. There were a pair of overstuffed, dung-colored chairs on either side of it, and in front of one of them, seated on the floor with his back against the sagging seat, was Neuville. His legs were stretched straight out in front of him, and he stared with wide, fixed eyes at the door. As Marius came in, he moved his legs as if trying to rise. Marius realized that this must have been the noise he had heard. He was wearing a white Mexican shirt with some sort of large, dark red design on the front of it, and it was only when Marius had taken a couple of steps towards him that he realized it was blood.

He stood appalled, his first thought to get out as fast as he could. After all, no one knew he was there. He had the taxi waiting, and could be gone in no time. He certainly didn't want to get entangled in an affair like this. But almost as the idea formed, he knew he couldn't leave. The man was still alive. And anyway, common sense told him it was too late for him not to be involved, for the cabdriver could describe him.

He squatted beside Neuville, wondering what he could do. The man had clearly been shot a couple of times in the chest. Marius could see the holes in his shirt. The man's eyes were filming over, his breath coming in slow gasps. There was bloody spittle on his beard. Marius looked around, found the telephone and reluctantly dialed 999.

He reported the shooting and gave the address. He

was in for it, now. He sat down on a straight chair, thinking, Why the hell does this kind of thing have to happen to me? and as he looked at Neuville the man's legs jerked, he gave a hoarse exhalation and his head lolled awkwardly backward. "Oh, shit!" Marius said, in a heartfelt tone.

He got up. After all, if Neuville was dead there was nothing else he could do here. Staying only meant he'd never make the plane. He started for the door, still debating with himself, should I or shouldn't I? The police would surely look for him, the cab driver would know him, and it occurred to him that Fitzhugh, who was connected with the police in a way, would know he had had some contact with Neuville. It would be worse to have the police searching for him than to get it over with. Even as he hung, still undecided, his hand on the doorknob, he heard the clatter of boots coming up the stairs.

He opened the door to two officers. Farther down, a couple of orderlies wrestled a stretcher up the stairs, preceded by a man in a white coat.

"This way," he said, standing aside.

One of the policemen bent over Neuville and then gave way to the white-coated man, evidently a doctor. The other policeman went to the phone.

Marius said, hesitantly, "Look, can I just leave you my name and address, and go? Here's my card. I have to catch a plane."

"I'm very sorry, sir," said the policeman who had been watching the doctor. "I'm afraid I shall have to ask you a few questions."

He took Marius's card and pulled out a notebook. "Hello, Forensic?" said the other policeman, into the phone.

"Is that your taxi downstairs?" asked the first one.

"Yes," said Marius. "I just got here. I was supposed to see this man on business and I found him like this."

"May I have your passport, please?"

"Certainly, but listen—"

A heavy footfall on the stair, and the door burst open. A burly man, hatless, bald, meaty-faced, came in. His gaze went from Neuville to Marius, and he said, "A-ha!" Then, to the policeman, "I'm Commander Wilde, C-13."

"Yes, sir, I know you."

"That chap's done for, is he?"

"Yes, Commander. Is this your pigeon?"

"I think it is. You're Sharkey, aren't you? Very well, I'll take this fellow with me. You'll know where to find him. Was he armed? Have you searched him?"

"No, sir."

"Get on with it, then."

Marius submitted as patiently as he could, only saying, as they opened his briefcase, "Please be careful of that, will you? It's full of important papers."

"Nothing, Commander," said the policeman.

"Right. I'll take that briefcase. Now, Mr. Kagan, if you don't mind, come with me."

It was on the tip of Marius's tongue to say that he did mind, only Wilde's face was so ominous that he simply shrugged and went with the other down the stairs and into the long, red Jaguar that was waiting in what now seemed to be a crowd of vehicles. Marius could think of nothing to say, and Wilde was silent all the way to his office. There, with Marius settled on a straight chair, he sat down, too, and carefully lighted a cigarette with a shiny new lighter.

In an easy, conversational tone, he said, "Well, Mr. Kagan, I thought I told you to stay out of my way."

Lulled, Marius said, "I wasn't in your way. I didn't

have anything to do with Neuville's death, I just happened to be there. If you'd waited to talk to that cop—"

Wilde's face suddenly went crimson, and he thumped the desk with a heavy fist. "That's enough!" he exclaimed. Almost at once, he controlled himself, the flush visibly draining away, like the blast of a sunrise giving way to the ordinary brightness of day. Then he said, "Let's not beat around the bush. Yesterday morning, that man, Guy Neuville, visited you at your hotel. You needn't pretend to be surprised. You're no amateur. Surely you know I've been keeping tabs on you. Tonight, you visit *him* and he winds up dead. Curious coincidence, isn't it?"

Marius, aghast, said, "But, good Christ, if I'd killed him, do you think I'd have phoned the police?"

"What do you take me for?" Wilde thundered, losing his temper again. "That's the oldest ploy in the book. It's a lucky thing my man didn't waste any time reporting to me tonight, or they might actually have let you go—such things do happen." He folded his hands in a clear attempt to get hold of himself. "There are several things I want to know. What have you done with the pistol? We'll need that. We'll find it sooner or later, anyway. More importantly, why did you do it? What does it have to do with the theft of the vase?" He tapped his clasped hands on the desk top. "You'd better understand, Kagan, that your connections aren't going to help you. This is simply murder, and I'll deal with it as such. But I want to know how it fits in with the snooping you've been doing. I mean to find that vase."

For a while, Marius could only sit in numb silence. Then he said, "This whole thing is mad. Look, I'm an art dealer. Neuville came to see me because he's interested in Chinese art. He took a piece of jade and left me a deposit. I went there tonight to pick up the rest of the money, and maybe sell him something else. When I got there, he was dying. What was I supposed to do, run off? I called the cops, even though I knew it was going to get me into trouble. I was planning to go to Paris tonight. What the hell else can I tell you?"

Wilde stared at him, and then, with a finger, drew a piece of paper towards himself. "You can tell me," he said, "why disaster has a way of following you. Do you know a man named Paul Li?"

"Sure. What about him?"

"You went to see him today, in his restaurant, the Mustard Seed Garden. You left him a few minutes before one. Half an hour later, a bomb went off in his office, luckily just as he was going down the stairs with another man. They were only slightly hurt."

"Paul? Bombed?" Marius's throat constricted and he could say nothing else.

"It's a surprise to you, is it? I'd have picked you up earlier, but I only got the information and put it together an hour ago. Well?"

Marius ran his hands over his head. "Oh, my God!" he said. "Where's Paul now?"

"Never mind Mr. Li. Something's going on, Mr. Kagan, and I want to know what it is. I want to know now, and no nonsense. You're in enough trouble already. I'll smash you!"

Oddly enough, Marius felt himself growing very calm. He had taken part in auctions in Japan, where the pressure was exceptionally intense, where things went very rapidly and one had to make instant decisions, and preserve, among the shouting of other dealers, an icy control. This was like that; the more he was pressed, the cooler he became.

He said, "In the first place, Commander, you're wrong about one thing. You said, before, that I wasn't an amateur. I am. I don't know how to make you believe me, but I'm not an agent of Central Intelligence. A lot of people have been making that mistake. I got into this whole business because Mr. Fitzhugh approached me and asked me to help him identify the vase when he found it. That's all I have to do with it. I told you all this once before, didn't I?"

"No," Wilde said, "you didn't. It's a good story."

"It isn't a story. It's the truth. I mean, you can get in touch with the CIA and ask *them*. I have absolutely nothing to do with the CIA or with any other organization. You can ask Fitzhugh, for Christ's sake. He knows."

Wilde opened his mouth, and closed it again. After a moment, he said, "Go on."

"Fitzhugh asked me to keep my ears open for any information, since I do move in the circles of the Chinese art world, and I have a lot of contacts he might not have —nor you, either, for that matter. I don't know how it's happened, but I've been sucked deeper and deeper into all this stuff. I think I know why Paul Li's place was hit. But it's got nothing to do with this fellow Neuville—how can it? I don't know anything about him. I don't know what enemies he had, or who might have wanted to kill him. I just happened to be there."

Wilde picked up a pencil, and with great concentration drew a circle on a piece of paper, put two dots for eyes, and a curved line for a frowning mouth. He finished it off with a few strokes of hair on top, and said, "You say you know why Li's restaurant was bombed. Well, why?"

Marius folded his arms. "I have a lot to tell you. But I'm not going to say anything unless you drop this crap about a murder charge."

Wilde's face began to suffuse with blood. Marius, who recognized the signs by now, said, quickly, "Hold on, don't go flying off into space. I plan to tell you everything, and when I do you'll see that there isn't any link with Neuville. He didn't have anything to do with what I've found out—or if he did, I don't know what it could have been. I wouldn't have any motive for killing him, although if I had the faintest idea how to go about killing anybody, I'd have plenty of motive for killing some other people, for instance, a son of a bitch named—"

He paused. Wang Lai's image had come into his head, and with it an idea so jolting that first it shut him up, and then made him laugh, although weakly. He waved a hand to still Wilde, and forced himself back to sobriety.

"I'll give you this for a starter," he said. "I know who stole the vase. A middle-aged, gray-haired man with glasses, a Cantonese—does that match your description? His name's Wang Lai."

Wilde grunted. "We found a pair of glasses in the basement of the museum. They had been thrown away by the thief. You're saying they were a blind, are you?"

"That's what I'm saying. Let me put it this way: Wang Lai is a middle-aged, gray-haired Cantonese with glasses who is certainly in this thing up to his neck. Are you interested?"

The Commander drummed with his fingers. What had told most with him had been Marius's saying, "You can ask Fitzhugh." He recognized the difficulty of someone in Marius's position trying to prove he wasn't with the CIA; at the same time, his only information on the subject had come from Fitzhugh. Wilde had been a policeman long enough to be able to judge the tones of a man's voice, and to discount them where necessary. Without fully relinquishing his skepticism, he began to feel that Marius was telling the truth. It was highly likely that

Fitzhugh had been playing one of those complicated games you could expect from the pinky-shirted twisters in Security. He made a mental note to have the fellow's head when this was over. Meanwhile—

"Yes, I'm interested," he replied. "Up to a point. I'll reserve judgment on the murder until I hear what you have to say."

"That's all I want," said Marius.

He began with his first meeting with Fitzhugh, and briefly and swiftly told the whole story, from his talks with Tashjian and Sun Chih-mo, through the incident with the Russians which he could now see in its proper perspective, his visit to Wang Lai, and his encounter with the motorcyclist. Only, when he told about Mei's role, he refused to mention her name; "a certain Chinese friend," was all he said, and when Wilde asked who it was, he answered, "Sorry, that's something I can't tell you. It would be too dangerous for—er—them."

He ended by recounting his last discussion with Paul Li, although he gave no hint that Li was in any way connected with any foreign agency. "He owed me some favors and didn't mind talking," he said. "He told me about this secret society, *Shih P'ang* it's called, Stone Circle. Sun is a member, so is Wang Lai. Sun owns the company whose truck was used as the garbage wagon. The Stone Circle—or anyway, Sun—has it in for the Reds, and of course as soon as I asked Wang those questions, he passed the information on to Sun and they decided they'd better get rid of me. They must have a spy in Paul's restaurant. Maybe he overheard Paul telling me about them. Or maybe they just guessed what I was after —who knows? I wouldn't be surprised if they tried for me again," he finished, with a shiver he couldn't suppress. "Anyway, it makes sense, doesn't it? It all ties together."

"Yes," Wilde said, thoughtfully. "It ties together." He had been making notes, and he leaned back, biting the end of his pencil. "This fellow Wang does match our description, and I agree it would have been a clever touch to leave a pair of glasses to throw us off the scent. There's no proof, of course. Perhaps I've misjudged you, Mr. Kagan. I won't say I'm sorry, because it's no more than you could have expected, considering the circumstances. Now, there is one problem."

He pointed the pencil at Marius like a schoolteacher. "Where do you suppose the vase is?" he said.

"How the hell should I know? It's wherever the members of the Stone Circle are keeping it. Why don't you just arrest Sun and Wang and make them talk?"

"Mm. That's precisely the problem I'm talking about. What I must do is recover the vase. The fact that Sun owns the company which owns the lorry isn't proof that he had anything to do with the theft. That complicates things. Leaving it aside, I can pick him up, all right, but that won't get me the vase, will it? I have to know where it is before I can go charging in and get it back. All they'd have to do is smash it to bits. That wouldn't save them, but it wouldn't help us, either."

"Yes, that's true."

"Now, *think,* Mr. Kagan. Was there anything—anything at all—that anyone said, which might give us some hint where it might be?"

Marius shook his head. "I can't think of a thing."

"Damn!" The pencil broke between Wilde's hands, and he tossed it aside.

Marius eyed him. The germ of an idea was beginning to form in his mind, something audacious, something which only he was capable of carrying out. Before he let it flower, he said, "Listen, Commander, what about that murder charge?"

The corners of Wilde's mouth drew down, following the doodle he had made on his pad. "I'm inclined to believe you," he said. "Maybe it was just bad luck your being there. However, I can't let you leave the country. Sorry, Mr. Kagan. I'll need your evidence, but in any event I daren't let you slip away until I know a bit more about the case."

"Then I'll have to stay in London, will I?"

"I'm afraid so."

"Ah, well." He thought of Mei. "There is someone I can stay with—"

"I suggest you don't. Don't even phone anyone. As you said yourself, if this secret society tried once for you, they might well try again. Whatever you may feel, I don't want you silenced. Whether we find the vase or not, you're part of my case."

"I'd forgotten about them. What'll I do?"

"We can put you into a little hotel where you aren't known. It'll do for tonight, at any rate. I'll see to it that you're protected. Then tomorrow—well," he continued, with an edge to his voice, "perhaps by tomorrow I'll think of a way to give those villains something else to worry about."

"Since I'm going to have to be here anyway," Marius said, "there's just a chance that I may be able to find out for you where the vase is. But it'll be a long shot."

Wilde gazed at him speculatively. "Go on."

"First, I'll have to explain something to you about Chinese art. I don't know whether you know anything about it—"

"Haven't a clue."

"Well," said Marius, slowly, "an important aspect of it is that very often things aren't what they seem to be . . ."

Chapter 13

It was a small, drab hotel, neither dirty nor uncomfortable although it somehow gave the impression of being both. A policeman fetched Marius's suitcase, and he was hurried from the car to his room, outside the door of which a man was posted; a second, he was told, would be in the street. He spent a restless night, between nervousness over what he would have to do in the morning, and a certain elation at having acquitted himself so well, on the whole. He remembered the strange lightheartedness he had felt so many days before, when Fitzhugh had first asked him to help, the sense of anticipation of adventure. He couldn't complain that life hadn't been exciting enough since then.

He was finishing his coffee, sitting beside the window, when he heard voices outside his door, and a moment later Fitzhugh entered, saying, "Good morning. May I come in?"

"Hi," Marius said. "Want some coffee?"

"No, thanks." Fitzhugh looked about the room. "Not exactly luxurious, is it?"

"It's okay. Have a seat. There's only the bed, I'm afraid."

Fitzhugh perched on the end of it. "So you didn't leave London after all, Mr. Kagan?"

"No, I didn't. I got into a mess. I suppose Wilde has told you all about that fellow Neuville."

"Not exactly, but I did have a man watching you, you know. Why did you visit Neuville? I thought you'd decided to take my advice and stay away from him."

"I wish I had. But he had left a deposit with me on a piece of jade which he'd taken, and I went to get the rest of the money. Well, but you know what happened to me, don't you? I had a long session with Commander Wilde. I had a hell of a time persuading him that I wasn't a secret agent who had knocked off Neuville because he had something to do with the Sung vase."

Fitzhugh nodded. In a tight voice, he said, "And how did you finally persuade him?"

"I told him everything I'd found out, all that stuff I told you. Then he could see that there wasn't any connection between the theft of the vase and Neuville's death. Why are you asking me, anyway?" Marius demanded. "You and he are working together. Why don't you ask him?"

Fitzhugh clicked his tongue impatiently. "Ah, yes," he said. "I thought I'd mentioned to you that Commander Wilde and I don't exactly see eye to eye. He has always felt that the political angle of the case was overstated, and he mistrusts my department. He didn't want me attached to him in the first place. So, you see, he doesn't always brief me properly."

"I get it."

Fitzhugh hoisted himself off the bed and walked back and forth restlessly in the confined space. He had had a bad night himself and had finished by drinking himself to sleep, so that he was not at his best. He had wasted little time with Neuville. He had had, first, to find out how much Guy had told the Chinese so that he could, if necessary, get in touch with his cutout, Sergeyev, and arrange to get out of the country in a hurry. He had pretended friendliness, had satisfied himself that Guy had not yet actually betrayed anything, and had then shot him. He had let himself out in a tearing hurry, and had evidently not closed the door tightly behind him so that Marius had been able to enter. Working it out later, when the news had come to him of Marius's arrest, he had realized that there had been no more than twenty minutes or so between his departure and Marius's arrival. It sickened him to think by what a narrow margin he had escaped being found. He had waited, then, for a possible summons from Wilde, not knowing what Marius might have revealed. His chief aim remained the same: now that he knew who had stolen the vase, he must protect them if he could do so without revealing himself.

He said, at last, "And now what, Mr. Kagan? Is Wilde going to let you leave the country?"

"No, he isn't. But, maybe I'll be able to get away by tonight if everything goes as planned."

"What do you mean, as planned?"

"I've got an idea for how we might be able to locate the vase," Marius said, not without a touch of smugness. "I'm going to see Sun Chih-mo this morning and try it out."

Fitzhugh drew closer. "What's the scheme?"

Marius hesitated. "It's too complicated to go into. I've got a kind of suspicion where the thing is. If I'm right, Sun will take me there. Wilde will have a man watching me, just one so as not to be too conspicuous, and when we get to the spot he'll tip Wilde off and the cops will swoop in. We've got to be very careful, you see, because as a last resort the *Shih P'ang* people could destroy the vase. It isn't what they'd want to do, for a lot of reasons. They're Chinese, and they have a lot of reverence for a fine antique piece, especially one with an inscription on it by an emperor. But if they were pushed, they just might. However, Wilde seems to feel that as long as they actually have the vase intact, they're in a position to bargain."

"Yes, I see that. You'll have to stall them, won't you?"

"I'll do my best," Marius said, glumly, as he had the night before when Commander Wilde had asked him the same thing.

Fitzhugh turned away to hide the spasm of pure fury which swept over him. He was in something of a quandary. He had come armed, with some vague notion of silencing Marius if he had not yet told Wilde all he knew. There was no point in it, now, and in any case he couldn't shoot him with the same pistol which had put two bullets into Neuville, and certainly not with a policeman outside the door.

The pistol—! It gave him what, in his present brittle state, seemed like the only possible idea. He would, however, need another gun. He had one, an old Lüger, in his flat, but it would take a little time to get there.

He said, "What time are you going to see this fellow, Sun?"

"He opens his gallery at ten. In about an hour."

"I see. Look here, Mr. Kagan. I think I know how you can stall most effectively." He drew out the Browning. "Take this," he said.

"A gun?" Marius stared at it in astonishment. "What do you expect me to do with that? I never even fired one when I was in the army."

"You won't have to fire it. If you take it out and point it at someone, he'll stand where he is."

"I suppose he will. Especially if I'm pointing it, because I'll be shaking like a leaf."

Fitzhugh still held it out, and at last Marius took it. "All right," he said. "Maybe it's not a bad idea. What's this little dingus on the side?"

"The safety catch," said Fitzhugh. He unlocked it. "There, it's ready. Keep your finger off the trigger, though. Just hold it, this way, and point it."

"I feel like James Cagney," Marius said, pocketing the thing gingerly. "You know what? It does suddenly give you a feeling of confidence, doesn't it?"

"Yes, it does," Fitzhugh said. "I must be off." He started away, and turned. "Tell you what," he said. "I'll keep an eye on you, just to be on the safe side, so don't worry about a thing."

"Why, thanks," Marius said, a little surprised at this unexpected solicitude. "That's great."

"Not at all," Fitzhugh said. "Good luck."

At ten past ten, Marius pushed open the glass door of Sun's gallery, and a faint buzzer sounded. Sun came waddling out of the back room. At the sight of Marius, a faint flicker appeared in his eyes, of surprise or alarm.

However, he said, with a smile, "Malius! How are you? I thought you gone away."

"I suppose you did," Marius said, in what he hoped was a properly steely tone.

Sun's face became impassive. He sat down behind the long table on which he kept his miniature garden, and said, in Chinese, "It is always a pleasure to see you. I suppose you have come for the Huang P'ing-hung landscape you liked so much?"

"Let's not waste words, Chih-mo," Marius replied, in English. "You know perfectly well who I am, and what I want to talk about. I've got some information for you."

Sun nodded. "I am listening."

"Mind if I sit down?" Without waiting for an answer, Marius brought a chair from a corner and made himself comfortable.

"In the first place," he began, "I think you ought to know that my people have no direct interest in this case. I know it looked different to you—that's why you steered me to the Russians, right? But now that I know they had nothing to do with it, I'm not interested. It doesn't really matter to us who has the vase if they haven't got it. After all, it's not a matter that concerns our security."

Sun clasped his hands over his belly. "Are you serious? An entente between the Red Chinese and Europe does not concern you?"

"Why should it? It will have no effect on the NATO alliance, except possibly to strengthen it against the Russians."

"But," said Sun, "you yourself were asking many questions—curious questions for someone who is not interested."

"Not so many. I had a chat with Paul Li, and I asked Wang Lai for a piece of information. I was repaying a favor for an English agent who is a friend of mine. That's all."

"And Madame Yuan? She is also a friend of yours."

Marius flushed. "Let's leave her out of this. My relationship with her is strictly personal."

"I accept your word for it," Sun murmured, skeptically. "And what is the information?"

Marius hitched an elbow over the back of his chair and looked about. On the walls of the gallery hung several paintings; on glass shelves, obliquely spotlighted, were a few choice things, a moss agate bowl, a T'ang horse, a disagreeably ornate jade vase.

"One of the things that makes dealing in Chinese art so much of a challenge," he said, conversationally, "is the amount of copying and forging that has gone on for a thousand years or more. You know that as well as I do. Take that painting over there—it's signed K'un Tsan, but you and I know that it's not a Ming painting but a good Ch'ing period fake. How many T'ang horses have you seen which really came from T'ang graves? Not many. It's an old tradition in China—the business of making copies or forgeries. It's not thought of as wrong, as we in the West might think; it's done very often out of reverence for a master, or to provide copies of famous works for connoisseurs. And you know how difficult it is to tell the difference. With paintings, the ink and paper may be the same over two hundred years or more. Bronze can be artificially aged and patinated. And ceramics—"

He paused, and his gaze met Sun's. "It's not hard to reproduce porcelain, if you have enough money and the right equipment and the right potter. It needs scientific tests—carbon dating, for instance—to tell the difference."

Sun's air of detachment had vanished, and he was looking definitely shaken. "What are you trying to say?"

"The Sung vase is a fake," said Marius.

"Not possible," Sun burst out. "They wouldn't—"

"Have you seen it?" Marius asked.

The other subsided.

"Well?" Marius said, sharply. "I don't want to fool around—have you or haven't you?"

"I have seen it, but I haven't examined it closely," Sun admitted. "Nevertheless, I can assure you that the one we are talking about is the one which was in the Adjai. And there is no doubt in my mind that it is genuine."

"You'd better have some doubt. In the first place, you are not an authority on porcelain. Your field is paintings, hard stones and bronzes. You don't know enough to say, Chih-mo. I've been informed that the Chinese government had a duplicate made, just because they were afraid of an emergency like this. The one your people took is that copy."

"I don't believe it," Sun said.

Marius sighed inaudibly. It had been a good try, but maybe it wasn't going to work. He went on, "Okay, suit yourself. It's got nothing to do with me. I was asked to pass the word on, as a neutral. They're your own people, even if you are against them. They want to give you a chance to save face. And of course, they'd like the copy back. It is, after all, a beautiful thing in its own right."

He waited; there was no response. "All right," he said. "On the sixth, the preview will be held as planned, and there'll be a vase on show in the case."

Sun's lips twisted. "How do I know that one won't be the fake?"

Marius shrugged. "I'm only a messenger boy. It seems to me that whatever happens, *you're* the one whose head is going to roll. And you and I were—are—old friends. You may be right, of course. Maybe they're trying to pull a fast one, and the vase you have is genuine. If so, you could use it to bargain with to even better advantage. If you could get an expert, I mean, an independent expert with no ax to grind, to look at it and testify that it *is* right . . ."

"You?" said Sun.

"Why not? What's wrong with me?"

"How can I trust you?"

"Why shouldn't you trust me? Any English or Chinese expert would have a stake in this thing. Not me. I think I can tell whether it's right or not. I'll pass the word on, and you can sort it out amongst you."

He waited for what seemed like a very long time. Finally, he made a move to rise. Sun waved him down again.

"We will try it," Sun said.

He took up the phone. When the answer came, he began to speak rapidly in Cantonese, of which Marius caught only a word or two.

When he had hung up, he said, "We go in ten, fifteen minutes. I ring up for taxi. Meanwhile, you like look at the Huang P'ing-hung, after all?"

"Sure," said Marius. "That's something I *am* interested in."

When, at last, they were in the cab, he felt a good deal of satisfaction and was able to tolerate being squeezed by Sun's bulk. Not only had the bait been taken, but his private guess seemed correct, for he had heard Sun give the cabdriver the address of Wang's shop. Marius had suspected that if Wang was the thief, the likeliest place for him to conceal the vase was in the safe in his own office.

He helped Sun out of the taxi, looking about furtively as the driver was paid to see if he could spot a police car, and reminding himself that of course Wilde wouldn't be so obvious. How long would he have before the cops came? Wilde had only said, "Don't worry, we'll get there," like a doctor telling a patient with extreme hypertension to relax.

They entered Wang's shop. The same sullen young man leaned on the counter over his *Playboy* magazine; a slow reader, Marius told himself. He gave Marius a quick glance, quirking up the corner of his mouth, and Marius suddenly thought, *I wonder if you ride a motorcycle?* Sun muttered something and the young man nodded and patted his jacket pocket. With a jerk of his head to Marius, Sun started down the stairs.

The mah-jong room was empty, but the tables were littered with tiles, as if they had just been vacated, and cigarette smoke still coiled among the overhead lights.

Wang Lai was waiting, unsmiling. Knowing what he knew, Marius could now see the hard planes of his face beneath that cheery, bobbing, slightly obsequious exterior. "Good-natured Wang" was a useful cloak, another mask.

"All right?" Sun said.

"Come my office," said Wang.

He led the way. Sun remained looming in the doorway, a cigarette between his fingers, while Wang opened the safe. He rose and held out a small bundle wrapped in a piece of soft brocade. Marius took it carefully. Wang stood back a pace, and Marius sat down under the hanging piece of calligraphy which read, ". . . righteousness is man's path," and turned on the gooseneck lamp on the desk. He unfolded the silk and took out the vase.

It stood no more than fourteen inches high, of a simple but graceful shape, as crisp as paper but strong. Its color was that luminous bluish-white called *ch'ing pai*, with a perfect, smooth glaze, almost alive under the fingertips. Marius turned it about. On one side, in the dashing and elegant hand of Hui Tsung, was written, "When shall we celebrate again in drunkenness?" It was a line from a poem by Tu Fu, a farewell to a friend.

Marius found that his hands were trembling. Only part of his attention was on the vase, for he was listening painfully for the sound of the police.

"What do you say?" Sun asked.

Marius looked up at him, and then at Wang. "Just a second," he answered. "I want to look at it through my glass."

He reached into his pocket and touched the butt of the automatic, checkered wood, warm from his body. Before he could move, however, a low voice outside in the gambling parlor said, "Stand still."

He recognized it: Fitzhugh. He saw Sun laboriously

turn around and caught a movement from Wang out of the corner of his eye. He plucked out the pistol and leveled it.

"Don't move, Wang," he heard himself say, thickly.

Wang held still, staring at him through his round glasses.

"Come out of there," Fitzhugh said. "Be quick."

Sun, raising his hands, left the doorway. Marius motioned with the gun and Wang followed. When they were both in the gambling room, Marius, clutching the vase to his chest, went out, too. Fitzhugh was on the other side of the room, a long-snouted Lüger in his hand.

"I know there's a rear door," he said. "Where is it?"

Silently, Wang pointed to a door in the wall behind Fitzhugh.

"Does it go to the street? Hurry up, or I'll kill you."

His voice had a note of such malignancy that Marius didn't doubt him for an instant. Neither did Wang, evidently.

"Wait, wait," he said. "It goes along cellar and up stairs to street. You go. We don't follow, I promise, I swear."

"Come on, Kagan," Fitzhugh said. "Keep well clear of them. Hurry up."

"Don't you want—" Marius began.

"I said, come on."

Marius edged past the other two and around one of the tables. Keeping close to the wall, he joined Fitzhugh.

"Go through the cellar and wait for me," Fitzhugh ordered. "Look for a light switch—probably beside the door."

Marius thrust the door open. A puff of damp air came to him, mixed with the faint smell of cheap incense and mildew. He found a switch and snapped it, and in the light of a couple of dirty bulbs set in the ceiling made his way between boxes, cartons, and barrels stacked on either side. He had taken perhaps a dozen steps when he heard the shots.

He stopped short, appalled at the sound, unable to believe it. A second later, Fitzhugh came into the cellar, closing the door behind him and locking it.

"What the hell have you done?" Marius said.

Fitzhugh was asking himself the same question. He hadn't intended to kill them. Harassed as he was, ridden by the fear of discovery, fatigued, hung over, he had made a hasty decision. He had planned to get Kagan and the vase away in the brief interval before the police arrived. That would protect his identity as a double agent as far as any of the members of the Stone Circle were concerned. He would then shoot Kagan, take the vase, and leave the American's body to be discovered with the pistol which had killed Neuville. Five minutes leeway was all he needed, but the pressure of time itself had been a strain. He had dealt speedily with the young man in the shop and had found the stair, but when he was actually facing the two Chinese it had occurred to him that they would be able to describe him to the police. How could he explain away Marius's death, or the disappearance of the vase, to Wilde?

And now, there was even less time.

He said, "I had to do it. One of them had a gun. Never mind that. Give me the vase."

Marius stared. His jaw began to shake, and he clenched his teeth with an effort. Then he said, "Wait a minute. How come you didn't want to wait for the police?"

"Give me that vase, you little bastard," Fitzhugh snarled, pushed to the limit.

The word *little* was unfortunate. Marius bristled. He was a dozen yards from Fitzhugh and he backed away still farther.

"I don't think so," he said. "I'll keep it until Wilde gets here."

He could see the glint of Fitzhugh's eyes and teeth in the dusty light. The Lüger came up.

"Have it any way you want it," Fitzhugh said, in a deadly voice. "I'd rather have the vase all in one piece, but maybe in the end it won't matter."

Marius sprang aside, behind a couple of crates stacked one upon the other. The roar of the shot, magnified by the cellar walls, was deafening. Splinters flew from the edge of a crate.

Someone tried the cellar door, and then a heavy weight struck it. Marius could hear muffled voices. He ran, bent almost double, along the narrow aisle between cardboard cartons. Fitzhugh fired again.

And all at once, Marius could go no farther. The boxes stopped at the cellar wall, blackened stone, fluttering with black cobwebs. He swung round, his back against the wall.

Fitzhugh was peering from side to side into the shadows above the boxes. He saw Marius and leaned a little forward to make sure of him.

Marius was still holding the pistol. Blindly, he brought it up and pulled the trigger.

Fitzhugh spun half round, firing at the same time. Chips of stone whining from the wall stung Marius's cheek. Fitzhugh dropped his own weapon, catching at his arm.

There was only one thought left in his mind: to get to Sergeyev and safety. He sped across the cellar, and as he reached the stairs at its far end, the door to the gambling parlor burst open.

Marius sagged, fighting to pull himself upright, swallowing the sour bile that had come into his throat. The pistol grip was as wet as if he had held it under a shower. Wilde came into the cellar behind a massive policeman, shoved his way past, and looked about, squinting. More uniformed men were behind him.

"I'm over here," Marius said. "The son of a bitch tried to kill me. He went up those stairs at the end."

Over his shoulder, Wilde said, "After him." Then he added, "Kagan? Come out."

Marius had to support himself against one of the cartons, but at last he made his legs move and came slowly into the light.

"Your face is bleeding," Wilde said. "Are you all right?"

Marius felt the cold wetness, then, on his cheek, and said, "It must have been a piece of stone. I'm okay. What about them?" He jerked his head at the door.

"Never mind them," Wild said. "What's happened? Who was that other man?"

"It was Fitzhugh," Marius replied.

"Fitzhugh?"

Marius held out the pistol. "Here, take this damn thing, will you, before it goes off again."

"Where'd you get this?"

"He gave it to me this morning. Said it would help me stall while I was waiting for you. But then, when he got here, he wouldn't wait for you. He made me come in here, and then he shot them. Are they dead?"

"One of them," said Wilde. "The other may pull through." He didn't seem very interested; he was examining the pistol. "The same caliber," he muttered. Then, to Marius, he said, "What about the vase? Ah, I see you've got it."

Marius had almost forgotten it. He had been cradling

it so rigidly that his arm had gone numb. He handed it over, and began flexing his fingers and kneading his muscles. "That was what he wanted," he said. "But why? Who was he working for? What was he—?" He thought again, and said, more slowly, "Was he on the other side?"

"Mr. Kagan," Wilde said, "did Guy Neuville ever mention Fitzhugh to you?"

Marius had taken out his handkerchief, and he paused with it at his cheek. "So that's it," he said. "Yes, he gave him as a reference. He said he could tell me some embarrassing things about Fitzhugh. There's another thing. When I phoned him last night, he told me he had had a call just before mine, from a mutual friend. I thought that was funny, but I had too much else on my mind to spend any time thinking about it. He meant Fitzhugh. And then, when he told me I could come at nine-thirty, he said that his other guest would be gone by then. 'Embarrassing things!' I told Fitzhugh that, too. I've just realized that Neuville must have taken me for a CIA man."

Wilde nodded. "I had the report on Neuville's murder this morning. They found the stub of a cheroot in the ashtray. It seems to me I recall—"

"Fitzhugh smoked cheroots," Marius finished.

"Yes, so do a lot of other people. Fitzhugh never would have occurred to me, because I wouldn't have imagined any possible motive. Not then," Wilde added, grimly.

He held up the vase to the light. "Rather pretty," he said. "I wouldn't have thought it was worth more than a couple of quid, myself."

Chapter 14

By the time they arrived at Wilde's office, a report was waiting for him that Fitzhugh had been picked up. He had gone only a little way along Lisle Street before fainting from the wound in his upper arm, and the two pursuing policeman had taken him to hospital.

"Can I be arrested for shooting at him?" Marius asked, anxiously.

"I don't think I'll arrest you just yet," Wilde replied. He was in high good humor, which manifested itself in a geniality so improbable that his subordinates kept staring at him. "You've done us a great favor, several favors. As long as you haven't slain the fellow, I think we can overlook a few irregularities."

He got on the phone at once, to report the recovery of the vase, first to the Assistant Commissioner (Crime) and then to the director of the Adjai, Geoffrey Foster. The Assistant Commissioner undertook to notify the Chinese Embassy.

"This office is going to be very full in a short time," Wilde hinted, to Marius.

"I want to be here when they come," Marius said, firmly. "Don't you think you owe it to me?"

"Yes, well, all right, Mr. Kagan. It'll be a squeeze but I'll stretch a point. Have to stretch the office, too, no doubt, ha ha."

He put a cigarette in his mouth and snapped his lighter four or five times without success. With a sigh, he tossed it on his desk and began looking for some matches.

"I'd like a full statement from you," he went on. "I'll put you in another office with a secretary and have you in when the others arrive."

"There's just one more thing," Marius said. "You never told me which of the two Fitzhugh shot was killed."

"The smaller one, what's his name?"

"Wang Lai."

"The other was wounded in the neck and chest. I don't yet know how he is, but I expect a report at any time. He's a friend of yours, is he?"

"Yes," Marius said, with a sigh. "I hope he makes it. I've got some unfinished business with him, a painting I want to buy."

Wilde raised an eyebrow. "Good heavens! I thought we policemen were supposed to be cold-blooded," he remarked.

Half an hour later, the office was as crowded as Wilde had promised. Geoffrey Foster, a tall, spare man with a permanent stoop, shook hands with Marius and said, "What are you doing here?"

"I'm a kind of friend of Commander Wilde's," Marius replied. Dr. Kao, who had brought the vase over from Peking, had a pudgy, round, innocent face and wore a handsome but ill-fitting summer suit; his companion was silent and solemn, dressed in a high-necked tunic of blue-gray. Dr. Kao was introduced to Marius, and they exchanged a few complimentary words in Chinese. Then Marius settled himself modestly in a corner, while the Assistant Commissioner chatted with Commander Wilde for a moment or two.

Wilde said, "I think we can finish the business quickly. Will you gentlemen please identify this property."

The vase was on his desk. Dr. Kao adjusted his glasses and bent over it. He straightened, smiling, and said in well-accented English, "Yes, this is our vase. No doubt of it."

"Very well," Wilde was beginning, when Marius stepped forward.

"One second," he said.

Wilde said, warningly, "Mr. Kagan—"

"Shut up!" Marius barked. He had been nerving himself up to this. "I have something to say. You haven't introduced me properly, Commander. You ought to tell them that I've been pushed around and locked up and shot at and almost run over, because of this affair. I never asked to get involved in it. It was only because a man named Fitzhugh made a slip. He told me when he first talked to me that everybody makes a slip, and he did, too—his slip was getting me mixed up in it in the first place. Well, I'm in."

He paused, with a belligerent air. Nobody said anything.

"The trouble with everybody nowadays," he went on, more quietly, "is that they get too hooked on *things*. Objects. Diamond-studded pisspots, solid gold airplanes. After a while, the things become more alive than the people who own them. You take this vase," he said, gesturing at it. "Commander Wilde's judgment was that it was pretty. We who know better know that it's marvelously beautiful, an ancient treasure, pure and exquisite, touched by an emperor. And so on. But really—" He looked from one to another of the faces before him, "It's just a vase, something to put flowers in. It's cost the lives of two men, the injury of three more, the reputations of others. Do you think it's worth it?"

He picked it up, so carelessly that Wilde involuntarily jerked out his hand.

"Don't worry," Marius said. "I've had the chance to study it. It's a forgery."

In the dead silence, Dr. Kao said, imperturbably, "You are right."

"Here! Just a minute!" Wilde exploded.

"It is so," Dr. Kao said. "You are very clever, Mr. Kagan, very good. We were afraid something like this unfortunate incident might occur, and so, a long time ago, when we knew that something would be wanted for the Museum of the East, we took steps to see that this replica was made. We intended, of course, to exchange it for the genuine one in time for the preview. I will not be so careless," he added, "as to go walking in the park with the keys in my pocket when the real vase is in the case."

Marius glanced at Geoffrey Foster, who said, a trifle defensively, "Yes, I knew about it."

"Well, well," said Marius. "And none of you said a word. I could have been lying on a slab by this time, next to Wang Lai. But of course, you couldn't take the chance that they might not try again, could you? And it would be best all around if you got this one back and nothing was ever made public."

"We were concerned for the safety of the real vase," Dr. Kao said, gently.

"Yes, sure you were. I would have been, too. I'm no better than the rest of you."

He was still holding the vase. He opened his hands deliberately, and let it fall. It dashed apart, fragments scattering and sliding along the floor under their feet.

"Oops!" he said.

LEE COUNTY LIBRARY
SANFORD, N. C.

Delving
The China expert